Archway Publishing books may be ordered through booksellers or by contacting:

Archway Publishing
1663 Liberty Drive
Bloomington, IN 47403
www.archwaypublishing.com
844-669-3957

Because of the dynamic nature of the Internet, any web addresses or links contained in this book may have changed since publication and may no longer be valid. The views expressed in this work are solely those of the author and do not necessarily reflect the views of the publisher, and the publisher hereby disclaims any responsibility for them.

Any people depicted in stock imagery provided by Getty Images are models, and such images are being used for illustrative purposes only. Certain stock imagery © Getty Images.

ISBN: 978-1-6657-2556-9 (sc)
ISBN: 978-1-6657-2554-5 (hc)
ISBN: 978-1-6657-2555-2 (e)

Library of Congress Control Number: 2022911432

Print information available on the last page.

Archway Publishing rev. date: 06/22/2022

Contents

Acknowledgements

The past couple of years, preceding 2022, were hell on earth for many; the loss was ubiquitous and universal. Few went through these years without losing something or someone; be it a family member, a loved one, a business, or a shop that was shut down by draconian measures implemented through tyrannical means and scare tactics without consent or approval. Whatever it may be, Charles Dickens knew this and so did our forefathers before him: when times are hard, we need a myth, a legend, a story, a fable, or a product of our imagination to get us through the day. I might have taken my characters to some extreme in this story, but the Aristotelian mean be damned! The priests are preachy, the knights are brave to the point of rashness, the kings are tyrannical, the lovers are mad - or at least some of them are. Few people are finding balance in their lives nowadays, driven to the brink of sanity, some have taken their lives and others have strengthened their resolve in their fight for survival. I hope you enjoy my fairy tales as they may get dark at a certain point, but I assure you, this is nothing new. Read any old fable by Charles Perrault or the Brothers Grimm and you will realize that, if anything, some of my fables are rather milquetoast in comparison. The only other matter that remains is to whom would I target this book? Everyone needs a reminder that some people exist to prey on you and others to comfort you. These tales are reminders that danger exists, and love exist as well even if one stopped believing in it, and that tyranny, like everything else, has an end.

That being said, I dedicate this book to my mother. I would not have written this if it weren't for her perpetual pleading for me to do something with all the spare time I had during the lockdown. God bless her and protect her from all harm - and for the rest of my family: my sister, brother, and father - I love you all.

Chapter One

THE COOP

In the beginning – and as the day reached its end and the horizon turned to a dark crimson pallet on the canvas of the firmament and the orange sun was setting beneath the horizon, a mother bird, a pigeon was she, lived with her three children whom she would always watch over. She was struggling to put her kids to bed, so she decided to tell them a bedtime story to awaken a sense of slumber in their being. They were a hyperactive lot, curious in their sense of discovery and eager to visit the world in all it had to offer. Their mother did not keep them in the dark at all. Some of her tales were those that brought joy and others induced dread and despair for her stories were those from what she had witnessed in her travels. She took it upon herself to tell them the tales that would prepare them for the life they were set out to live and it was not always sunshine and rainbows that were preceded by torrential rain, sometimes the thick fog blinded their sense of direction and other times the sky was so cold it could free the feathers from their wings. Life had a lot to offer, and these stories were the best way they could fly through the world, metaphorically at the very least, before they could spread their wings.

"Once upon a time there was a human mother telling a story to her human children, a family just like ours. It was a story about beautiful colored birds, like us, but different in their eyes for we all looked differently to other beings." Her singing voice carried out these words with grace.

"Does the story have a happy ending?" asked little Robin, the eldest, yet his flapping wings could barely carry him off the ground. He was the most distinct-looking bird. For every time the care-taker tried to cut his nails, he would make a debacle out of things, running and flying around the room to escape. He did not fly well even though he reached an age where he should. The youngest did not fly at all and had to ride on his mother's back whenever they wanted to fly.

"All endings are happy endings. I do not know how it ends my dear, but if it ends badly, we have no one to blame but those who weave us into existence through their words. Have I told you about the spinster goddess Nit?" she asked.

"She tells all tales through her weaving fabric, and her evil sister, Apropo, cuts the fabric and then things die!" responded Robin. The mother smiled. Her stories did not fall on deaf ears. "You make it sound like a bad thing. All things must come to pass and the only way she could have enough fabric to weave life is through cutting off another, but you must have faith in our mother, no harm would befall you as long as you uphold her commands. Recite to me youngins, as you have done before, the prayer that has been passed on to us once more."

"Mother, may your thread last me

One more night and day
Mother, to you I humbly pray
not in a grave, but in a bed
tonight, let my body lay." They all recited the prayer by heart.

"Good children," she pecked them each a kiss on the forehead. A moment of dread befell her, her words muted beneath a shivering beak. She could not live without these little birds. If a feather on their wings would come to harm, it would be the end of her. Six years was their lifespan, and six years they would live, she would often claim.

James was the youngest bird. "Mama," he said. He was incredibly silent for a kid his age. That did not mean that he lacked a sense of wonder and intrigue in this world, but he was aware of his speech impediment through his peers' constant reminder. It did not matter what they said. They, after all, served the humans, and the humans did not understand a word they said. "Go on," he continued. The middle child, Rosy, was the most silent. She sat warm and cozy between her brothers. They have always protected her and kept her warm and in return she gave them guidance, despite being 3 weeks old. She was not only the wisest, but she also knew how to fly, a fact that always put Robin in a state of dismay, since he was two weeks older than her. His mother had taught him well not to envy his sister, but to learn from her. Mother Sue took a deep breath, then narrated.

"Once upon a time, two kings were at war. One had an iron fist, four of its fingers were the kings' and the pinky was the clergy. He could do without it, but it was a useful accessory at times. He always clenched his fist, dictated rules, and ordered his subjects to be loyal rather than earn their loyalty. Through his fist, people started to slip, and their trust was broken. Many of his subjects pleaded, 'Please sire, a fist could not be shaken by another hand but shakes on its own, the results of your most recent brash actions could not possibly end well.' And they did not. His kingdom was indebted to ten others and his people were stricken with periods of famine and the constant scorn of their neighbors. With every battle won, another was lost, and the war advanced very little with the sands of time falling fast enough that many could witness the walls of the castle crumble into pebbles. Every stalemate and every advance were equally banal. A day the trumpets blew in indication of victory, but when the bodies were rolled within castle walls and the wails of their women grew louder in volume than those of the instruments, it made their victory as much as a reason to rejoice as defeat. There was turmoil in the hearts of his subjects, but their faces were blank despite their rage. The king ruled over his kingdom while fear reigned over the people [...]"

"Mommy, could we not have a happy story for once?" cooed James. "I do not want evil to win again. Are humans evil? Are all of them evil?"

"Bah!" interrupted his uncle Larson barging into the scene. With every step, the cage rumbled. He was heavy and spoiled; the princesses' favorite. He was still swift despite his size, and never has failed to deliver letters from or towards another place. "Evil? asks my naïve young nephew who fancies himself for some flightless bird," he paused, looking at Robin, making sure his insult came through as clearly as possible. He did love the little ones. His demeanor was just naturally mean towards all. Some called it tough love, others abuse. He got Robins' attention. "Everybody is evil, son. Everybody is capable of doing evil. Thus, everybody is evil. Potentially, of course, but when potentiality exists it only takes a certain factor to bring it about in one form or another." He turned around maniacally, "I have seen pigeons eat other pigeons!"

"What are you doing?" She held their ears closed with her

wings, wishing she could turn back the clock just enough so they could unhear these words.

"Introducing them to world, my dear, to its suddenness and abrupt interludes of violence. Just wait and I shall tell them about their father's fate." He looked at her in earnest eyes. "I know nature made us for one partner, beautiful Sue, but you need to make peace with the fact that yours is gone."

"He will be back. I know it in my heart, and I am willing to travel to see him with my own two eyes."

"Travel," he scorned, "to the war-torn Westland."

"I know it, and I'll prove it"

With those words coming out of her beak, he bowed and left her to tuck her kids to sleep. Each pigeon had a bed of its own - so warm and cozy. "Big day tomorrow," she kissed them goodnight, "sleep well my loves."

The general mood within the cage was bleak without words signifying those emotions of despair and uncertainty that existed nonetheless. The glaring exception would be the King, plotting ever so heartlessly within his hall not too far from the room in which the caretaker and his subjects lived. Every quarter in the castle, though a physical space, denoted the King's priorities. His hall was the largest, a gathering area which was seemingly infinite. The more one looked towards its end, the more it extended out of the reach of their vision. The sun made its way through the stained glass that depicted his military expeditions, each an Odyssean feat that ended in an inevitable victory for the King who was an erudite, well versed in all subjects of the trivium, but did not care much for the moral repercussions that might follow from his actions. Outside, the grey arch buttresses were befitting the most beautiful cathedral, climbing into the heavens and curling back into the walls. Thirty steps below were the kitchen, another thirty and the caretakers' room, no bigger than a cottage with a low roof and claustrophobic space that seemed to be closing in on each other by every passing year. It always smelled horrible no matter how well ventilated it was, it's unfortunate placing above the stable was to blame.

The pigeons revered the caretaker Francis with every ounce of their existence. As a matter of fact, the caretaker was a figure in their religion, yet not deified, a man sent by the goddess herself. He would serve them, and they would serve in return, not only him, but the kingdom and its entire people. A sad little cripple was he, with a tattered beige costume with a tear from overwearing it. He was certainly hygienic; however, the same costume would smell flowery day after day, but he owned none other than that which covered his nakedness. A simple man was he, but not a simpleton, he learned politics from overhearing the King, and philosophy from overhearing his brother, a learned man, and for a man of his stature in society he knew far more than he had the right to know. He turned around to watch his birds hopping and cooing in their cage and smiled, his mouth pushing his drowsy, darkened eyes upwards. He had lost sleep during the last few nights. His brother was a priest, one of the Godfearing ones, thus, he was hated by his fellow men of the cloth for he reminded them of their corruption, and he was equally hated by the church goers, for he reminded them of their cowardice. Day by day, his frustration grew equally with all that surrounded him from the weak knees of the masses to the empty heads and inflated chests of the King and his men. Today was the day, he thought, he would have to be the sacrificial lamb. One major difference between the lamb and himself was that the lamb knew not it when it would die. Ignorance was the greatest of gifts bestowed upon man, but man rejected it wholeheartedly. He was Abraham and Isaac one in the same and he waited for the Lord to crack open the sky and tell him to sheathe his knife and sacrifice another. He walked, a priest and a warrior, in defiance against all. Moira had its peak, and it was at the castle gates.

He walked with long strides and a passion that burned like a wildfire, calling all those who toiled their fingers in the land until they faded. He reached the castle gate. The townsfolk listened as he spoke as his voice was loud and it echoed far enough to reach the King. He garnered quite the gathering.

"I address this to you my lord, may you listen and listen well." The King walked away from the throne and leaned his head out of the window. The priest continued, "If I prick you with a knife do you not bleed? And does fear make you not deter? If you are human then, which you are, how do you not err? Your majesty! You are wrong, and you do us wrong by not heeding our cries, resign your crown to another and let him bring us justice. You are not taking advantage of these good folks' gullibility but rather mistreating their goodwill, making you not clever, but treacherous." The townsfolk who rejected his call gathered around him unconsciously, not to defend him, for his scathing criticisms and his controversial sermons made him a disagreeable fellow. Perhaps, they just wanted to witness the theatrics that would ensue imminently.

"Silence!" The King's voice rang as loud as the church bells, a voice just as demanding of his attention. It was a warning he did not heed.

"You may moderate my tongue, your highness, but you shall not moderate my mind. My spirit elevates beyond the laws of any man, and in the hereafter, it shall float in a realm beyond yours. I know you to be educated enough in theological matters to know what I mean." The priest paused and lent him a gaze accompanied with a pestering grin.

"Your impudence will be your demise, boy. Guards!" He

ordered the armored men who listened attentively to this grand debacle. "Take him away." The men scattered momentarily, more than happy to oblige and obey the old man in the chair. They have reduced themselves to their armors, an inanimate thing incapable of critical thinking.

He fought with all his might but failed. He was outnumbered and not in his best shape for he has been fasting so that God would give him the strength and courage to go through such an ordeal. He saw his hands in shackles and turned, aiming his gaze directly at the King's fiery eyes. Their eyes met, one wanted peace and the other war. "The despair I feel could writhe my bones and twitch every tired fiber of my being, knowing that my father died for you, in other words, for nothing. You have spared us, foolish usurper, me, and my simple brother, spared us, and that was your last mistake." They shut his mouth with dirty cloth and wrapped his body in chains, an iron ball followed his steps, lowering his foot and shortening his stride, his motion was akin to limping. The ball followed still, every cling and every clang, with every push his leg was pulled, if luck and the divine would favor him, this ball would follow him to a cell, if not it would follow him to the grave. He did not care; he had a smile on his face as he listened to the whispers of the people with pitchforks and torches growing louder. He looked at the stars and prayed for the good God with a silent tongue for things not to escalate. Darkness came taking over the skies and the moon was at its zenith, the tired people of Vorwahl finally started to express their dismay; their anger conducted like howls in the nights' sky, the King knew he had to appease them. At first, he appealed to them through his authority demanding them to disperse. They would not bulge. He then resorted to pleading and still they would not move. Things went out of control, torches flew and created a fire that could not be contained before it could further cause damage. Many things, the precious and the inexpensive equalized, reduced to ashes as they went ablaze, smoke coming out of them, like a final façade before the fading shapes burned to ashes, very soon little possessions would remain.

The cripple, held his head between both hands as if he was going to lose it, from his brother being arrested, to the rising of the mob, this all could not bode well. He smelled the smoke, then, momentarily noticed the flame climbing, creeping to his chamber. In panic, he thought about carrying the communal cage, but it was heavy and even though he could carry it, it could be perilous in case he fell, and the pigeons became helpless betwixt the iron bars. He rattled the cage to awaken the birds, they all jumped as they arose from slumber, perplexed for being awakened in such a manner. Francis never stirred the cage unless there was reason to, and there seldom ever was. Languor accompanied them, they usually flew all day, if not doing deliveries, then just celebrating being alive for the ability of flight, reaching a distance that shrunk the world beneath. Francis opened the cage and carried Larson in a hasty manner, strapped on him an anonymous "red seal" letter delivered to him by a shadowy, bony figure, then released him into the wild, making way through the smoke safely. The others dispersed quickly on his command and made way to the cherry tree outside the gates where they witnessed an enemy faction besieging the castle.

Francis wiped the tears from his cheeks and attempted to clear the smoke that veiled the world from his window. His squinting devilishly red eyes spotted the birds landing in the designated area. Seeing no way out for him, in great panic he jumped through the window and landed in a fiery haystack reserved for feeding horses. He rolled onto the ground, then swiftly made way to the stable to guide the horses outside.

The emergency bells rang and the townsfolk that felt the

addressed his subjects in a manner so stern and so stiff that they had to stop. At once, their legs were glued to the floor when once they were tapping, and their mouths shut when once they were yapping. Noise, so much noise gone that its echo too vanished forthwith in the silent night.

"I forgive you," he cried dramatically. He then started pointing at the townsfolk with their muddy shoes and beer-stained clothes; they were always clean except in times of festivities, war, and toil and travail. "You," he pointed again to a target unknown, who had at that moment forgotten the pint in his hand and gulped his bile in fear. "You. You. Maybe even you, treacherous fiend. Do not bother to interrupt me in asking for forgiveness for you are all forgiven, like a messiah, my judgement is fair despite my might. It seemed like minutes ago when you were trying to make this castle my grave and I rise above it, and I rise above your pettiness. I built these walls, not to protect me but to protect you. I sent your men not to serve me, but to serve you, and despite it all, you want me gone. Why?" His voice changed from fear mongering to one that beckons pity. "My men are your men, and yours are mine, if you were not loyal to me, then," he opened his arms, as if inviting them to come closer as he addressed them from above, "Who would be loyal to a king not his own? I do not ask for your loyalty or love, nor would I demand for those are things you cannot force upon another. But know that I need you loyal and loving, and I promise," he growled, "I promise you shall need no one else but me. Serve me, and in turn let me serve you." They hailed the King, raising their glasses to heavens and praising his majesty before his retreating silhouette disappeared. He raised an arm in acknowledgement, not of their praises, but of his plans going just the way he wanted. A sly smile accompanied his footsteps as they echoed in an empty hall.

The knight exposed his horse, his only companion, sitting

silently on his knees in the vast wilderness. Faint music played and a crowd danced to it. He took great offence knowing this for he saw it as if they were dancing on the carcass of this nameless body; this nameless child he called a foe. He prayed one last prayer and gathered the courage to walk back to the halls of the King. Doubt was boiling on a slow brew in a concoction of forbidden thoughts; he had to silence his mind for the mere remembrance of the last uprising against the monarch and the fate of its individuals sent shivers down his spine. "Adapt and survive," he whispered to himself, such he had to do until the old man met his fate.

He pushed through the crowd. The drunken dancers could not see well but they could still identify him, towering above their heads. "Sir Sebastian!" The maidens bowed, and so did the men who knew him. He was a tall fellow, firmly built. He had blue eyes and pasty white skin, for his body barely saw the sun without the armor. He had seen many a battle and was unfazed by the ordeal of murdering a foe. He thought he had a cause and that was his loyalty to the King, but doubt was well nested in him now, and he could not outrun his thoughts. Much to their dismay, he ignored everyone around him and marched straight into the hall of the King.

"The armor is unlike anything I have seen," exclaimed the knight in anger, complaining to the king, "the people are from an exotic faraway land. Complete strangers have become enemies now. It is the last thing we needed."

"Do you reckon you know where they come from, Sebastian?" asked the King glibly. He took all those who fought as simpletons who took orders and asked no questions. Perhaps, he could sense the knight was onto something, so he had to know what he knew. Sir Sebastian did not have a single expression drawn on his face. He was quick on his feet outside of battle as well. He decided to play the fool, the good knight who lived and died for chivalry.

"If I were to take a gander, I'd say they were just mercenaries, sire. They fought under no banner, the scum." He doubled down on the act; he was no expert in thespian affairs but could act just well enough. "A man who fights for no country, a man who fights for no maiden, a man who fights for money, is a man of no honor. Thus, I do not regret my only kill. I am happy to report they have retreated swiftly, the craven bastards."

"My dear knight, it is a pleasure to have a commendable warrior of your stature on our side. Do you have anything else to report, anything at all that bothers you?" asked King Edward. His skin was elastic, wrinkled to the point that it could separate from his flesh with blowing winds, white hair flowed from his face veiling a part of his visage, he was in a pitiable state physically yet his ornamented, gold-plated armor covered every inch of his body. It was hard not to take pity on the man in question, but his lust for power made it hard for people to have pity.

"Nothing, sire," replied Sebastian.

"Be on your way then, and God be with you."

Sebastian bowed and left in silence as a war raged within him, a thousand words he could speak, a thousand condemnation to the old man's recklessness and disregard to everyone else. Yet, nothing could come out him. He was brave enough to confront him, but habit has had its way with him, and it was a knight's duty to follow orders, as foolish as they were.

He walked out and stealthily a shape of a man tiptoed into the scene; a lanky figure dressed in silk that had enough power to order soldiers to die for their king at any moment, for that reason, and for his infinite cowardice and physical weakness, he never saw eye to eye with the knight. The King was respected for once. He fought ferociously and with passion for glory, his old age caught up with him now and he knew that the only way to win is to resort to the intelligence of his advisors, as devious as they were.

"My dear Charles," ordered the old man, "You have heard the knight, have you not?"

"Yes, my lord," hissed Charles behind the king's ears, moving to face him, "What should we do about this problematic individual?"

"We need to confirm our doubts. Send our best spies to watch him closely, I want his every move noted down at all times."

"Wise decision. Consider it done." His laconism in times of peace came in heavy contrast for his constant blabber in war, as if the thought of people dying invigorated him.

"You are the one knave that scares me the most, you really do make my skin crawl."

"Why so, my liege?"

"The timing for the letter was far too impeccable, I thank you, the fool in the watchtower, I even extend my gratitude for the pigeon for being so swift."

The standing snake took a bow and turned to slither away.

"One more thing before you go," ordered the King.

"Your majesty?"

"How much should we pay for that poor child?"

"Don't lose sleep over a commoner, your highness. I would say the plan went facilely if it weren't for that one bump in the road. But if I were to put an estimation on his head, I would say his life would not be worth than a hundred silver coins."

"Make it two hundred."

"Right away sire. Anything else?"

"Do you think the people noticed anything suspicious?" he asked in a tired voice.

"It is impossible that they would think as we do. We are the finest minds in the kingdom pit against plebians, whilst we plot for years ahead, their minds are preoccupied with the redundant daily routine of toiling, working the field, washing clothes… Things cattle would not consider wasting time on," he said condescendingly. The King looked at him in disgust, ordering him to leave. Charles bowed and disappeared into the blackness of the hall where he prepared to reimburse the cost of life for a hundred coins, another hundred would fall, incidentally or accidentally into his pockets, or so he would reason if caught for the lack of a better explanation.

The King was left on his lonesome in a dark hall ornamented with memorabilia from conquests and relics from fallen foes, asides from what few gifts he has received as treaties of peace. The floor tiles were black and white, on it a rectangular red carpet lays on the floor beneath his step all the way to the entrance. Its crimson color had reminded him of a violent past that never left his memory and kept him on guard for all his life, for as long as memory would serve him, and that was not too long ago. Above the grand entrance, an extravagant oil painting, a masterpiece of art portraying a poor child. His youth apparent and so was his agony. It was concealed beneath a thin blue transparent coat, but the colors were still vivid and so was the figure; it depicted a snowy background to his unclad upper body as the rest of him was submerged in snow. His arms were holding his blackened shoulders as if in fear of them falling off. Many of his subjects saw this painting as they were leaving the castle grounds. In his earlier years, they saw this as a way of him looking out for the destitute and keeping them in sight and in mind. Later on, as his interests in his loyal subjects waned, they regarded the painting in utter disdain; they considered him a sadist who enjoyed looking at the less fortunate and found pleasure in seeing their pain.

His chair in which he sat for countless hours listening to plebians, paupers, and princes alike was a work of magnificence. The armrests had a head of a dragon carved on both sides. He would often grab them and squeeze as hard as he could for hours each day with his right hand, missing its smallest finger, an activity he engaged in now as he was left alone to his thoughts. The candelabrum struggled to stay alight. The candles that stood upright in a past not so distant were now formless, molten matter that were struggling for breath as they burned themselves to death. Wind blew inside the castle somehow from some hidden crevice and the fire danced to its rhythm, a silent symphony wheezing through an overlooked crack. The King pondered about his subjects turning. It was not an impossibility anymore; it has already happened if not for the mercenaries he hired as stage actors, the kid who died for naught was a curse, a precursor of worse things to come. He sat on his throne for hours staring into the void, a contemptible sound in his head repeated some whispered chastisements passed around like gossips, but the words amplified in his skull, "it is cowardice to start wars from the safety of the castle gates". He had many vexations now, many a concern raised between him and his loyal subjects whose loyalty waned by the second. He had lost sleep. The ability to slumber with a peace of mind was now a pastime that could only be remembered. He set his eyes skywards and read the carvings on the roof:

> From the things that life would send
> how many sighs, and joys, but alas,
> the beginning always predicts the end
> that this, too, shall pass.

> The dry, sunbaked dirt
> washed away with the rain,
> and times shall invert
> moments of pleasure and pain.

Snow too shall and will fall
and so will the leaves descend.
It is such, and such with all
What comes to be must end.

That which you look at,
(and that which you see)
is not what you remember,
the blemish of memory
shall be torn asunder.

I have seen the gleaming sun
in many a rendition
yet, the sun remains as one
such is the human condition.

And with time, you shall remember,
and with time you shall also forget
if your fate has been sealed
or it has already been met.

The dormant volcanos and dying trees,
the final flight of aging bees,
people came, and people went
time wasted, and time spent.

And all that came to be will go
leaving with nothing to show,
buried beneath time's sinking sands,
or a clock with a frozen hand.

Empty words and deaf ears,
silence echoing through the years,
mute thoughts awaken you in bed,
a word unheard is a word not said.

Whatever fate you have faced
from love and gains and loss,
the shadow of man was replaced
by the shadow of his cross.

So, cease the day, or cease it not,
things you remember, things forgot
stone and iron will not last
when it's time that comes to pass.

Outside, a lone mercenary slept, shivering as her fire died, and the golden feathered birds laid not too far away for the smell of smoke was too repulsive for them. It was unanimously decided by all to sleep outside and keep a single guard awake. The winged elders rested still under the moonlight. Larson mumbled to himself, "Guard duty, again. I got to stay awake, it is a special day for the upcoming generation. Yes, very special indeed. Big day tomorrow. Stay awake, Larson, stay awake... Oh! Where is my brother when I need him? I need my sleep. I need my sleep!" Sue awoke to silence him, claiming he was caterwauling too loudly. Her tired eyes demanded the nictating membrane to open, but they did not budge, she watched Larson hopping on a branch above beneath the translucent layer. "Shush," she whispered.

"I'm sorry princess, get some sleep. Your children have a big day tomorrow."

"A big day indeed." She proclaimed with pride and hesitation,

"I hope Robin gathers enough courage for it, I know he could make it, yet he doubts in himself to a crippling extent."

"I know he could make it, and so will he in time. Trust me, it runs in the family. While I have bested my brother, he in turn bested everyone else in the tribe. His superior genes will kick in when the time comes."

"You think so?" she asked. She had no doubts, but wanted affirmation.

"Look around you," gently whispered he in a tone lower than the passing faint icy winds. "The other contestants do not stand a chance. Not at all. Victory is guaranteed. Susan's children are bullies, and we would be better off without them."

She grasped in disbelief, "take it back, you mean spirited vermin."

"Hah!" he laughed. "You hurt me with your words, lady. You know I jest."

"Some jests are cruel you know; these jokes could be directed towards my little hatchlings."

"You forget by tomorrow that they will be hatchlings no more, Goddess willing."

"You're a good bird, Sir Larson," she said laying her head on her chest and gently closing her eyes. "One that needs to shut his beak and think well before opening it."

Larson smiled and watched them lay silently as their feathers danced in the breeze. He must not sleep, so he averted his eyes from the slumbering crowd and to the lone warrior. Her fire was reduced to ashes, but one was alight within her. They all witnessed her mourn the unknown fallen, solemnly weeping upon his carcass. He watched her closely until the first rays of sun started to shine from afar; individual fiery blades granting sight to a blind world.

He thought to himself and remembered a sermon from the revered priest who now could not see the flaming star blessing the earth.

"You will wake up one day and see it all as a battle between good and evil, when you reach that point in life you must always remember that evil has won battles but never wars. Battles that could cost you your life, your sons' lives, your loved ones' lives, with no exceptions. Accept your loss with grace, especially the loss of material wealth that you would accumulate. The rich man shall not and will not see the gates of heaven for his greed knows no bounds and his weapons causes many sins. When the swords could lead to murder alone, the coin causes adultery, bribery, greed, and at times entire wars, and we all know war is where man goes to die thrice. At first he kills his humanity, then his body, then his soul. It is hard to imagine so round and blunt an object; so small and insignificant in its dimensions that causes so much damage, not only in this life but in eternity, condemning so many souls to a fiery pit. When the Pagans had the obol to offer Charon, carrying it beneath their tongue so that they would be granted passage to Hades, our lord was generous enough to lead us there for free, if only we were unfortunate to fall in sin.

When our mother Eve was tempted by the snake to eat the apple, we knew we should not condemn her, but the snake. We rest assured now in knowing our mother Mary stood as victor over the snake. The reptile is our enemy. As mammals, it is due to fear, and the fire that comes out of its mouth is too a cause of fear. But we must slay it. We must slay the dragon, not to get to the gold that it guards, but to triumph over its evil, and the gold that it guards is there for the common good. The gold is not literal, friends, nor is the dragon, but when a knight walks into the unknown with a map that says, "here be dragons," it does not mean that he does not put his life in danger, the dragon is very much there.

Indeed, I say to you, I never put an armor on my scrawny figure, nor have I ever carried a sword, but I saw a dragon. I saw a dragon in the depth of the night when I was accompanied by no one, and I thought that this was my last trial, after it there would be no more. But the sun then shone as it promised it would every day, and the dragon disappeared into the darkness. It was then that I learned that it was the shining of the sun is good, God is good, and the son of God is goodness. Amen."

The man who spoke those words was now imprisoned in an underground cell, entombed in a manmade abyss; the cold and dampness of which could cut through his flesh, his bones, and his flesh once again until nothing of him remained. The putrid smells and the blind dark within, one could think he was already dead. Through time, illness could reach him before judgement came, but for the time being he was alive, and as long as he lived, he was at war. He was subjugated to suffering, torture, humiliation, and anguish, but it was okay for this day has come to pass. Knowing many other days like this day would follow did not bring despair but hope for there would be another day to live, to see what few rays of sun could seep through the cracks above, to pray for the lord once more. It kept him going and it kept his heart beating despite it skipping an occasional beat.

A distant light was growing closer. The silence was interrupted with the sound of a torch burning the invisible atoms, closer and it closer until a face could be seen behind it. The hair was covered in a dirty, rusted chainmail coif, its metal links spread to his chest, and the rest of him was iron.

"This is it, you old delusional fool. This is how it ends; this is the alpha and omega and everything in between," spoke a young voice.

The priest took a long look at the face but could not recognize it. His gaze could not pierce the darkness to identify all the colors that were alight. It was foggy, too foggy. His murky vision could not make out the shapes. Straight lines were moving, dancing with the faltering fire in his hand. He did not speak a word. He had a calm and collected composition. He knew this man was the torturer, if he were to suffer, he would suffer in silence. He remembered an old sermon of his, "a complaint to God is one taken into consideration, a complaint to man is mere humiliation.

Chapter Two

INITIATION AND TRIBULATION

The day has come. All the little birds that spread their wings in practice now had to be put to test all they have learned from their elders. The trials were dangerous, merciless in their design, but the obstacles were made this way so that they would offer a true challenge for those who undertook the path of the messenger. The pigeons awakened at first light. They were looking forward to this day, a medley of emotions within them turned their anticipation into the frantic confusion; it was the same as the first flight of their hatchlings in the excitement of watching them soar into the boundless blue sky. There was an ever present danger of them not being ready, and excitement would be replaced by terror and dread as the inheritors of their bloodline came crashing down into the earth. Some predators volunteered to offer their guts as a temporary grave. They were in a state of frenzy. Every single one of them, even the eldest, Melvin, could not bear the thought of their numbers decreasing yet again. This rite of passage came at a cost; if they were to pass, they would be a royal subject with all the privileges that came with that honor, if not, more often than not they would die and their bodies would be lost. If the goddess had more thread to knit into their lifeline however, they would return, but they had to be exiled and left at the mercy of mother nature, a fate inarguably worse than death.

Within castle walls, festivities were brewing, the bard sung, and the people danced as they awaited the arrival of the King. He could mandate laws and put out orders at his heart's content, but there was one thing that still had power over royalty and their crowns and that is tradition; a law unwritten that could cause the masses to erupt in anger if broken, like a sacred seal. Everyone had a role to play, tradition dictated, and everyone will play that role, dictated the masses. The King had arrived at the scene, carried on his throne, his face lacked any symmetry that could signify enjoyment. The caretaker came along with a drowsy disposition. He spent the night cleaning his chambers from the fire and its aftermath. He foresaw a past time augury, an omen undoubtful in its prediction that one of the beings he loved best would have to perish today, there never was a time where all survived, every time he would hope, pray even, that maybe this year would be different. His heart has finally given up on hope and all he anticipated was death. It was better that way for him. It was better to expect none to survive and be proven wrong than having his impossible optimism shattered; his fragility made him as irredeemable and as useless as broken glass. The pigeons showed, as their wings spread and their figures grew bigger and nearer and the flutter of their wings louder,

the crowds cheered, and festivities grew jauntier. The bard sang a
little song, his surroundings sang along:

> The letters of these words
> are delivered through my tongue
> but these birds deliver
> some letters unsung.
>
> Many a danger shall they face
> out there on their own,
> yet with calm and with grace
> they claim the sky alone.
>
> So, we put to test
> the skill of the bird,
> it is by no means a jest
> to carry around a word.
>
> A burden so great it is,
> a simple test would show,
> ask any bored wife, any old Mrs.
> for then you would know.
>
> A word unknown, not of your own
> is a thing of danger.
> Man could not let a thing he's met
> and leave it as a stranger.
>
> Those who survive the trial
> whose little hearts are fierce
> in their wings we pierce
> deservedly, there's no denial.

A golden feather of a yellow shine
if you'd believe these words of mine.
An article if I may be blunt
worth more than me or any old runt.

So may the best man
or is it the best bird?
May the best messenger
send the word.

As for these words of mine,
a product of cheap wine,
shall cease, for I shall not sing
the final word belongs to the King.

The crowds cheered on the bard as he bowed, politely asking them to stay silent. It was time for the King to address them. They all listened diligently.

"Faithful subjects, we are gathered today from miscellaneous walks of life. The sun has already left us, hidden above this sudden grey cloud, but by no means must this inconvenience ruin our festivities. Even if it were to rain, no downpour shall perturb us, we will stand firm as always. Tradition is sacred, and these beings bond us in a way we will never understand. Without further ado, let us begin." The King cued Francis to release the pigeons into the wild, and they flew, their little hearts beating faster than they have ever experienced, rapid thumps like tribal drums raged within. This was the point of no return, they either flew, died in an obstacle, or imposed exile upon themselves. Flight was imminent on the caretakers command as he shooed them away.

Rosy called Robin to stay with her at all times, she repeatedly encouraged him, and he was pleasantly surprised with her newfound supporting demeanor. He was at first circumspect of his sister's sudden change in attitude, for she had always scolded him alongside Larson, but now, with both of their lives were in grave danger. "Do not worry, brother dearest. I know you can handle it. I can see you already are out of breath. You need to exert less effort on individual strokes, but you must move your wings fast. Less power, more speed. Stick with me and watch very carefully." She gave an exact physical demonstration of his fault and tried to reenact it before dropping in altitude.

"Any slower and I would fall, brother. Show me what you have learned." He had doubts he would manage so quickly but he did. He was pleasantly surprised with this sudden progress.

"I learned it so quickly," he said, turning to his sister with a smile.

"You were born to fly like so, you nincompoop," she giggled, watching closely as her brother's flight has changed just as drastically as her manners.

"Good, very good!" she noted cheerfully. "Now fly closely. We'll get through it all.

Outside the festive atmosphere, their wings carried them out into a panorama that offered nothing but desolation. Dangers from all angles presented themselves so suddenly and swiftly as if regurgitated by a vortex. The trials consisted of a series of maneuvers that the pigeons had to successfully go through. Within the abandoned castle hanging from its roof was a pendulum, wires of thorns suspended from the moving hinges, an abomination that was part nature, harmless in its structure, but the other part was manmade from rusted broken swords, deeply embedded within the vine-like graft union, camouflaged in its brownness, it swung back and forth unceasingly. Within the empty spaces of the vines lay many a bone from the pigeons who were unfortunate to die in the first trial, filling the void between the wooden fiber in a way making it less of a hazard for future partakers. All they had to do is avoid the many sharp blades dancing in the wind. Alain and Eileen, Susan's children, and Eshter and Eli, the widow Eleonore's children, also made safe passage. There was a neighboring school of pigeons who underwent the same initiation trials, all were unharmed as well. Sixteen young pigeons entered and all sixteen left. The witness rode his horse to the King to deliver the good news.

Second trial commenced imminently. They had to descend in an underground tunnel filled with mud and muck, worms and snakes, and frail walls that could collapse at any given moment. The echoing hiss of the slithering fiends welcomed them as darkness surrounded them. It was a test of might, perseverance, and bravery. Few could escape their predators. Here, there was no sign of pigeon carcasses, and the reason was obvious; it was time to feed as far as the snakes were concerned, and their prey were delivering themselves at their own will. The malicious mischiefs knew that these recurring ceremonies would take place. They did not care what the purpose of these trials were. They had made of this day an annual banquet. The numbers of their flying meals have been decreasing on an alarming rate, those who escaped notwithstanding. They decided to make it harder for them and what was designed to be a straight tunnel by the humans have become an underground maze. The reptiles have outsmarted the mammalian bipeds and their feathered pets.

They rode the cold wind above the slithering horde as the snakes hiding behind the darkness sang:

> I am the son of the mighty dragon.
> I am the son of the mighty dragon.
> I shan't eat the filthy humans
> put their bodies in a wagon.

I am the son of the mighty dragon.
The god that breathes fire.
I am the dragon's son.
Do not test my ire.

I am the dragon's son.
My will shall be done.
The knight is gone.
The night forlorn.
Tonight, we shall be one.

I will eat you, little bird.
I will enjoy your taste.
Before your final word,
tonight, you will be waste.

The intertwined bodies twisted into a combined coil stretching, weaving a hostile menace of many eyes, as if a uniform being gazed and saw into the blackness of the underground. Picky monsters they were, choosing the plumpest bird to swallow and in that order they would feast. They saw the little winged things struggling, hitting into walls, and falling. Many were swallowed already and went without a sound, without a warning to others. Rosy's wings have started to fail her, as if fear had a body that sat on her back encumbering the wings with mental baggage that could not be shaken off. Fear paralyzed her. Motor functions began to stagnate, as if she was certain she was going to be eaten so her mind decided to fail her before her demise. Robin kept going, if he had not inherited the aviation skills from his paternal ancestry, he certainly did inherit their bravery. He went through the maze with little worry about his fate. He was as blind as his peers but still had faith in the goddess that she would provide, somehow, she would provide. Robin and his sister stuck close together, and even in his blind state, he could feel her wings faltering. He called to her, but she did not reply. As her body was beginning to lose elevation, he sensed immediately something wrong and grabbed her by his uncut claws; they slightly pierced through her flesh, but if that was what it would cost to save her, he thought, it's a little price to pay. He dropped slightly in altitude, but he had to persevere or perish.

"Rosy," he called to her, she would not reply, as if intoxicated by the poison of the fiends below before they could reach her. "Rosy!" he called again firmly and loudly, "I know you are hearing me, nod if you hear me," he could feel the motion of her spine beneath his foot signifying she had life in her. "Good, I want you to pray, there is nothing else to do but pray right now. The goddess will provide, I know she will." And there was light, faint light hanging like a string, guiding their way through the maze. He did not know where it would lead, but he was more than happy to see, more than happy to follow. Spotting the angry eyes of the cold-blooded fiend between and beneath the muscular scattered strings did strike some semblance of dread in his heart, but hope had overcome all evil, and the light gave him the faith he never had. He joined his sister in prayer and the brightness intensified, so did the buzzing of the insects' wings. They were fireflies! A lot of them, and they had no reason being underground unless the goddess wanted to intercede to their prayers.

"What are the imbeciles doing here?" hissed an unknown enemy.

"Eat them! Eat them all!" another replied.

"We don't eat insects," the third one spoke.

"It doesn't matter, if you don't take out the light, they will escape the darkness. Do not allow them to escape." They started flying around Robin. Their gnashing teeth missed his wings, at times caught a feather or two. He had trained for this scenario before, avoiding the perpendicular splashes of the water fountain within the castle walls. Robin still had no fear; he followed the faint greenish glow towards the exit, after many twists and turns they have arrived at safe ground. The sun was not there to greet them. There was more downpour than when they have entered, but rain was a preferable alternative to the fangs of beasts.

Rosy came through. Her eyes took in the sights around her, slowly and gently she arose. She could feel tingling pain in her back. "It was a bit of a sticky situation, but I managed to save us both," Robin said with pride, standing not too far away from the hole through which they have escaped. Rosy's awakening was sudden, but she could still see behind her brother a hungry snake slithering silently, her tongue muted by the pitter patter of rain, and before she could warn him, he was swallowed whole.

"Robin!" she screamed into the thundering sky, lamenting the loss of her brother. Time stopped. The sands in the hourglass did not fall but held their ground suspended midair, shock, and terror took over her. She had managed to fly to safety on a tree branch but the one who saved her was gone as instantly as a drop of rain reached the ground and vanished. She wanted to cry horribly, this loss was too sudden and too unbearable to digest. The fatal vagaries of nature had presented themselves to her at the prime of her youth; they caught her off guard and swept her off her feet. Before bitter tears could hit her cheeks, a falcon cracked the clouds with his shriek, he descended with the speed of light, the ground shook upon his arrival. As the snake sprung carrying his victim in his throat, spewing deadly paralyzing venom from its tongue, the gold feathered apex predator watched the oversized worm with delight, the way one watches a furious child threatening him. The falcon wanted to see the snake looking at him, he wanted the

like a waterfall on an open land. "Friends! Six have left, three have returned, we could either sit in silence to mourn the fallen or rejoice with those who are with us. I suggest we celebrate today and mourn tomorrow. But if this decision was not symbiotic and agreed upon by the majority, it will be revoked at once. All those in favor of a celebration say aye."

"Aye," the voice overcame the silence of the despairing dissenters. The families of the fallen withdrew from the festivities while others prepared. There were little leftovers from the banquet, but it was not enough. They broke into the bakery and stole all the loaves that went unsold, and into the brewery they flew and carried with them all the ale undrunk. They sang and danced all night long. The rain demanded attention, falling on their heads, bodies, food, and drinks, but it was ignored through and through.

In the pit of a jail not too far away, a man stripped of cloth mumbled to himself a past sermon. The water droplets distilled from the muddied ceiling and onto his back. His body was scarred and bruised, drawn onto it an unknown map that symbolized his misery and pain whose whereabouts were within; it was all courtesy of the torturer. A single water droplet fell, and like a paint brush. It went through the lines highlighted by the illustrator as if it were to revise and draw upon them once again. The droplet made its way through the scar like a river, condensed with his bodily fluid, it emerged differently. It was no longer water, it was blood, and he swam, submerged to his waist in the freezing red pond with hands tied above his head. His body was numb and frigid, his head burnt with fever, and his tongue moved beneath shivering lips.

"The world would be a better place if we could see how others suffered. But the cost of suffering was too great, forcing too many of us to close our hearts to the pain of others lest we are driven mad by despair. We all suffer have our trials and tribulations, and we all want to help, in theory, but in practice we all fail.

Consider Job.

Job was a good man, a good servant, and a man who loved God, so they all said. But if you obey God to gather riches and if you obey God thinking this is a pact with the Almighty in return of faith you hoard on wealth and property, it does not mean that you love God! It means you love the works of man! The glory of man! The vanity of man! You must work for the love of God alone, God and God alone! Prosperity be damned. Our ancestors were stripped and burned in the name of the faith, in times of peace, now we use the lord's name in vain.

If you worship God for prosperity, I expel you this instance from this sacred ground, to leave and to never return. Do not love God for what he could give but love God for he had loved you, for he had made you, and for he had sent his only son to die for you. Love God for what he had given you.

The godless claim that we are a product of chance and circumstance is not one that brings despair. It only strengthens my resolve; it means I have even more responsibility in loving my neighbor and more responsibility in loving God and his likeness. This responsibility has grown in magnitude to which it has become a burden so great if carried it makes a saint out of the carrier. I dare not claim to be myself a saint, but if my words could make one out of you, I shan't be proud of this accomplishment for pride is the greatest of all sins, but I would be lying if I said my joy would not be rapturous. Keep in mind that the pain that life brings, constant and ever-present, is with only abrupt interludes of joy. Until then, carry your cross and keep going. God be with you."

Some steps on stone slabs that echoed in the chamber came closer and closer until they stopped. "This is the point in your life where memories start. Take hold of you for the past is and will be all that remains from you. Your foolish sermons are falling on deaf ears, always unheard or actively being forgotten," interrupted the torturer, biting into an apple, masticating. He spit out the following word, "I will lishen to you, your worthless life leshons, pleashe do tell for I were told that I was a brilliant lishtener."

"I regret nothing," sighed the priest as he spoke aloud. His lungs writhed in pain awaiting his final breath.

"Do you hate me?" asked the torturer, swallowing the fruit.

"Why would I?" he answered in the dark.

The torchbearer laughed quietly, "am I losing my touch? Are you not in pain?"

The priest gazed into his fire with calm, "I cannot complain."

Chapter Three

VOYAGE

The knight journeyed outside the walls for a short saunter to a place yonder. On the other side of the walls, a woman lying on the ground next to her campfire whose shades of black over-shadowed the emerging flame. She sat on a log, a hollow facsimile of a former self unknown to him. He had sent one of the pigeons earlier in the day to deliver the torturer a message regarding their rendezvous, a message in which he offered him money for a favor. Bribery was punishable by death to any official involved in clandestine dealings, even those who were not involved in such matters were forbidden to receive a single coin that was not theirs. But there was a price for the crime that had to be paid, and for the man he considered a father, he would pay in full.

He saw the torturer hiding under a distant tree, yet not far away so he could see him. Without thought, as if instinctually, he took off his coat and placed it on her back. She did not look at him in gratitude, but her gaze fixated upon a flame that burned no more. "What is your business, m'lady?" he asked worrisomely. She did not refuse to answer, but her mouth would not open, between the bruxism and the chattering teeth, she seemed like a tramp far away from her home; one who was not beggarly enough to find shelter from by passers nor resourceful to seek it on her own. He would leave her to deal with the fiendish fellow awaiting him, but he promised himself to return to the helpless maiden. His footsteps crushed the snow below him and the sound accompanied him every step of the way. Crunch after crunch, the snow too deep to see the dirt beneath.

"Ahahaha," the torturer sardonically remarked with his baleful laugh, clapping at the arrival of the knight, "how gallant, how chivalrous, how heroic is this tin man. Oh, fear not, ladies, he is metal from the outside but pink and soft from within. Where is your armor anyway? Have you forgotten it with the blacksmith?"

"I am going hunting," he signaled to his bow. The mockery went past him as he replied in seriousness and amusement abated from the torturer's face. "Who is she?" he pointed to the woman who hugged his coat as if it would bring her more warmth. Her white face was growing whiter still, enshrouded by the snow beneath.

"I have heard rumors of her son dying in the siege, some other rumors insisted she was with the mercenaries who besieged the castle, but they abandoned her here for some unknown reason. But you know how it is, lies are spread like wildfire while truth is buried in an unmarked grave or a blank tombstone. She does not matter, knight. Focus." His eyes pointed to his open palm, "you have something I need."

"You torture an honest man. Do you have no vexations from your foul actions? You bring him harm, yet you seem unfazed and in good humor. Do you not think of what you do to be abhorrent?" asked the knight to the torturer handing over a full bag of gold coins.

"Absolutely not. It hinders my performance. Say what you will, but I have never killed, I do not kill on command as other people you may be well acquainted with would. By acquainted with, I mean you really, really know, as one would know oneself," he replied while shaking the bag; throwing it up and down to estimate the weight and content of the bag. "You look at me as if I was some repugnant dog. One day you'll learn that we all have a price, dear knight, and that includes yourself. I am a slave to gold and you to your ideals, and who knows, one day it will be the end of you. Stop thinking yourself to be better."

"I make an active effort at becoming better, in case I fail I know that I tried," replied Sebastian in a wearisome tone. Witnessing Tobias count his gold with a grin from ear to ear confirmed his biases about the man. The torturer to him was the lowest of the low, the kind of people who made the world a rotting pit, a drop of mold that one had to dispose of before it spread.

"This may seem shocking to you, but I do not care the least of what you do and who you are," he paused, "Mr. Tin, we have ourselves a deal." He offered his hand, but it was left unshaken. The knight turned to the boundless white canvas to see a convoy of slavers whose cage stood out as it was covered with a black piece of cloth. They grabbed the unsuspecting victim who was morphing into a sculpture of ice. She could not fight, nor could she scream. Her body was carried and easily disposed within the bars of the wheeled prison. The knight witnessed the abduction and ran after the peregrinating menace. The torturer's laugh reverberated like a white ghost amidst the pale land. With a swift draw of his bow, an arrow bolted through the back of the captor's neck who rode lonesome on his horse while his companions, two they were, manned the carriage. Upon the fall of their comrade, they panicked and hurried, begging the horses to go faster as if they would listen. The knight pushed the body off the steeds' back and rode, he chased the criminal couple urging them to halt before firing a warning shot next to their ears, but they would not listen. The chase went on.

Above and slightly beneath the clouds, a mother pigeon flew with her children accompanied by a falcon so majestic. Their genuine golden wings, though they shone beneath the silver sky, were singular. Every feather on the falcon was naturally golden brown, and each wing was the size of a pigeon in its entirety. He had a spot of white feathers on his neck, crop, and breast that went along nicely against the whiteness of winter, fluttering with the chill breeze. If one was to look above, they would notice him and him alone, and if one were to listen and listen carefully, the mother's soft coos were harsh words scolding her careless children.

"How can you 'forget' a thing so important? We have been waiting for news about your father for an entire season!" Sue reproached her. James sat silently on her back, featherless and freezing. They dressed him in an unfinished yellow yarn cloth stolen from the castle. Though his bones danced from the cold, he was in an indescribable state of glee to leave the confinements in which he lived his entire life, young as he may be.

"I would fully take the blame, mother; my brother was in a dire situation at the time, and I would not be shocked if memory failed him about details regarding that day," Rosy defended her eldest brother.

"If there is one thing I remember, it would be that day and that moment. I just forgot to say mother, maybe I was carried away in the festivities. I did tell you that I was about to lose my life," Robin pleaded

"If you think you could silence me with guilt, you are wrong," she reaffirmed them of their mistake.

"What were we to do anyways? Fly in the middle of a stormy night? That does not seem wise at all!" explained the eldest child.

"I dare say he is right," said the falcon. He spoke from his throat as calmly as he could, but it was just as penetrating as his shriek. "If you don't mind me interrupting..."

"As a matter of fact, I do mind" she interrupted him. "My husband has been gone for too long and anyone who knows anything about his disappearance owes me some answers. Is he ok? Please tell me he is unharmed," she begged him to speak.

"We promised not to disclose any information of his whereabouts, or his conditions," je abstained from telling more than he was permitted to tell.

"He is injured! I know it, I just know it. Why would he not fly back?" She was increasingly worried with every word spoken.

"Relax. He is alive and that is all that matters," the falcon replied.

"I thought you would not disclose any information on his conditions?" asked Rosy enigmatically. She wanted to know about her father, but she was conscious of their companion breaching his pledge to her father in such a short time.

"It is a small price to pay for your mother to lend us some silence. Hush now. We have got days' worth of flight; I suggest we save our breath to save our skins."

A feather fell from the falcons' coverts and onto the torturer's head. He rode for long on the shimmering glow of the glossy white garb nature has made for itself, ruining it beneath the weight of his friendly beast. He scrubbed the feather away from his chainmail and looked above to see a speeding winged platoon on an unknown mission. He made his way to the prison, which was outside the city walls, for the bodies were buried together in mass atop of each other while the higher ranked persons, the priests and the wealthy, were buried closer to the altar of the church. It did not matter to him where or whether he lived or died. He lived bereft of hope and joy or any other emotion notwithstanding hate. Nothing would give him satisfaction which made him claim time and again that God would do him a favor in stripping his soul from his body whatever his fate may be in the afterlife for there he was promised joy or sorrow for all eternity. If more nothingness followed him beyond the pale, his lips would fail to complain if after death nothing remained.

He was greeted outside the entrance of the jail with two lardy gentlemen, one an excessively corpulent fellow who looked like an oversized cannonball; his head was another smaller one attached to it. His companion also fleshy, like a pump round bird, yet significantly smaller than the other priest. They wore brown pieces of cloth that took days to knit; not for the colors or complexity of the design of the attire but for the sheer size of it. They both wore shapeless reddish-brown robes that were hyperbolized upon embracing their bodies. They walked around with smiles on their faces as if they were carved in marble, a curve that did not denote nor insinuate inner peace or unity with the divine but rather the same countenance would be found on any wild fox upon encountering a pen of helpless poultry.

Upon noticing the contours of the bloated figures from a distance, the torturer hurried his horse. He squinted his eyes to reaffirm what he saw, and his presumptions were reaffirmed. It was truly the priests whose pockets were just as inflated as their physiques. He smiled, he knew some coins would be thrown his way and in return he would promise the sadists something false, a lie, the illusion of compliance to a treaty that was conceived from fantasy in the hope and faith in another. He had no faith in another. He saw himself a figure of darkness, a shadow, who had no obligations. Swearing and promising meant nothing to him, his ideals were different and nonexistent. He had no goals other than the destruction of others' ideals.

He disembarked his beast and walked to the people in brown. They introduced themselves as soon as he approached the gate and slipped the key into its hole.

"I am Cecil, and the fat fellow is Felix, and we are more than pleased to meet the infamous torturer," the smaller figure spoke.

"Tobias, it is an honor to make your acquaintance," the torturer spoke, forcing a smile. "I think you are unfair to your friend since he outweighs you only slightly. Whatever happened to gluttony as a sin?"

They took no offence to his scathing words, "it is writ to do as we say not as we do."

"I find it hard to take a man seriously if he did not live by his own words," he replied instantly.

"You are observant, cunning if I may say so. I would like to ask you what you are doing in a field that takes mere physical prowess, but I digress. See, that would be counterintuitive for the purposes of my visit. I carry gifts with me." The priest opened a bagful of gold, maybe twice what the knight has offered, but Tobias was unfazed by the glitter, at least outwardly, "gifts are only what a smart fellow would appreciate, a fellow who knows what matters in life."

"What would you like in exchange?" asked Tobias

"Our 'brother' to disappear," he answered.

"Murder? You ask too much from me, father," he remarked sardonically.

"Oh, it's too little for the price paid. Too little indeed. More would come your way once you have evidence of you doing your part. Come now, Felix, let our friend sleep on it. Mail us when you have a lifeless carcass in your hands, then you will dine with royalty."

The torturer was accompanied by his steps, hollow thuds of his foot hitting the ground one leg after the other. He threw the full bag up and down. The clink of coins he had amassed filled the air, and in turn filled his heart with joy indescribable. He laughed like a madman in the night of the prison, for on the sunniest day, the light did not penetrate the stones of his abode. He hid the gold in a chest of his. He kept it in his room then headed to the cell in which the priest slept upright; his arms wrapped in chains nailed to the walls. The water surrounding the priest was a frozen crimson pond, he was a figure so pale the jailer thought him dead. He rushed in opening the cell and hurried to break the ice and free the man from his confines. His collapsed body so cold that it hurt to touch him, if he himself could feel the frost on his skin he would cry in pain. The torturer was afraid. He held a cadaver between his hands and his promise to the knight was about to be broken, but there was a pulse faint and frail, the priest despite the odds would prevail.

He transitioned the arctic body to a cell with a mattress on its ground and a hole in its ceiling from which light would barely enter; the rays would glimmer on his glittering skin. The torturer covered the nakedness of the body with the warmest coat in his acquisition and lit a fire close to him. He sat next to the soon-to-be corpse and told it tales, some he had heard, others he had witnessed, few he had imagined. He begged mercy to the unconscious prisoner, he even confessed many of his past sins knowing well he would not gain absolution.

A maiden lays as the priest lays next to the fire, and the knight sat upright like the torturer sat. The great white veil of snow sat still upon the lands surrounding them. He looked at her. Her beauty obvious was to him; she could not hide it no matter how hard she tried. Her cheeks like a blossoming rose in a season a flower would wither and die. He could not help averting his eyes to her feminine wiles and she noticed him noticing her. She was still in captivity, while not too far away, the bodies of her captors laid stiff and buried in snow, a shallow grave nature had provided. She was still in her ropes struggling to move. Sebastian looked at her, waiting for words of gratitude, perhaps even an apology.

"I'm glad you're having your fun, but you can untie me now," she exclaimed.

"Not until I hear some kind words coming out of your mouth."

"T-thank you," she struggled to speak those words, "now." Her eyes pointed towards her bindings. The knight got up and cut the ropes around her body. She was angry with herself, allowing herself to fall captive, to be as helpless as she was, to now be indebted to a stranger.

"I refuse to be saved by the likes of you," she said. She stood up and started to walk away.

"For the longest time, I had refused the fact that I was born. Yet here I am. If reality could adapt to our fantasies, the world would be chaos, but it is not. Listen to me," he followed and grabbed her shoulder to stop her, "It's perilous, it's cold, and you will die. If not a prey to man, a prey to nature you would be, of that I am most certain."

She turned again away and walked some more until she had made up her mind that a companion wouldn't hurt, safety truly was in numbers. She looked back and motioned with her head for him to follow and he was happy to oblige.

He walked in silence. He walked behind her in distress. Could she be the mother of the child he had struck down? How would he confess what he had done? Would she forgive him? How would she forgive and why? He had to give her reasons and reasonings. His mind raced. What could he say to her to make things right? For the time being he walked in silence and hoped she was not whom he thought she was.

Chapter Four

LOVE IN THE AIR

A black, unsuspected pigeon made his way above the castle gates. He had found the caretaker within the walls, or the caretaker had found him and immediately gave him shelter amongst the other birds in their new pen. Francis hurried to King Edward and gave him the letters with the different seals, knowing who it was from. The King immediately took a deep breath. He needed patience whenever she corresponded with him. It was the Countess of a land far away, his cousin some would say but it was a disputed claim for the King had no family, no spouse, and no children. The usurper's claim to the throne was a legend whose facts were altered to fit the view of those who documented his reign, whose documentations were falsehood and untruths for their words were paid for. One thing was certain, he had truly killed the previous king and took his place, this truth regarding regicide was undisputed.

He pressed into his eyes and squeezed as if he would somehow unread the words on the scroll. He called to Francis and demanded he would send an elder pigeon, one experienced in flight and knew the given route, for the pigeon who has arrived did not know where to go. In the pen, the bird in question identified himself.

"My name is Shaw. I have come from the far away walls of Calistero. My prior is dead, and I took his place."

"You're far away from home son," exclaimed Melvin, "how does the Countess fair?"

"Quite well. I would have sent the letters to her husband myself but with great shame I inform you I am ignorant of the route in question. I never fared to the war-torn woodlands."

"That is no shame at all," he whispered, "by the by, all our females are looking at you the way a scribe would study a text, or an alchemist would gaze intensely at his potion. A shame would be if you were to lose your life for a piece of paper. Tell me, are you married son?"

Shaw was startled at the intimacy of the dialogue. He stuttered, for he was a stranger who was met with an unsuspecting degree of familiarity. He would still humor the old bird.

"I am single, I'm afraid. I have spent a great part of my life in the air with a piece of paper warming my chest from the incoming winds. I can't say I regret a single second of my travels even if my personal life suffered from it."

"Oh, how I agree," Melvin exclaimed, "we are born to soar up and above, beyond the petty squabbles of these humans, but I can't help but be loyal to them, as if my nature conspires against my a priori need to be free."

"I know this feeling well, friend. I know this very well." Shaw shook his head to this sentiment. Melvin smiled, he showed him around the pen and gave him the names of the faces he saw. Once he reached Eleonore, Francis lifted her up in the air and attached to her a letter with a pink seal on it.

Eleonore was carried away with the blowing wind and she flew alongside it as if she were integrated fully with its invisible symphony. Beneath her laid a sheet of snow which was melting as the sun had arisen for days before. Mud, water, and frozen ponds looked up at her passing by. Her fluttering wings strong and firm, devoted to her purpose in being a courier, a messenger, an animal who was worth at times more to humans than their fellow humans. There was a theory to the humans, it was of course unconfirmed, but it boggled their minds for a long time. The birds carried the pink sealed letters and the lavender sealed letters, even the yellow sealed letter at a speed tenfold of that when they carried a red sealed letter. Of course, it was not always the case, but in their paranoia, those who speculated exclaimed that the birds could understand their magisterial code and were wary of the small animals, constantly giving them suspecting looks and in return, the animals would gaze at them with an intensity that some would call idiotic, but they saw it as cunning. Eleonore flew away; away from home, the speeding arrows, the soldiers and their clashing swords, and sickness and disease-ridden tramps who walked this world without a home, without shelter, without hope. Filth-ridden marauders and blood-washed soldiers would look up at her as if she would be their deliverance, as if she carried a message that would calm the raging storms in their souls; be it from a mother, a father, a wife, or a loved one in this cruel unsympathetic world, but she went by them, feeling sorry for them. She could do nothing but watch as she sped by them.

The two-day journey has come to its conclusion. She had reached the garrison where constable Krill spent his nights sleeping and his days giving orders for the lower ranks, for that is all that mattered here; ranks. The faces did not matter. The missing limbs did not matter. The dead bodies did not matter. Orders trickled down from above, and those below were expected to obey blindly, deafly, mutely, and idiotically. The earl marshal barged into the tent of the encampment in which the constable laid his head, obscure behind the many pillows he had, next to him was a fluffy white cat. The marshal hesitantly shook him awake, and the first thing his waking eyes beheld is a pigeon. He scattered the blood-stained blanket, changed into his gambeson and sat on his chair dismissing the marshal, and opened the letter which was dampened as it flew in the melting snow and morning dew.

"My Dearest Love,

The moon is above hand, yet it feels within reach. Its white glow reflected by the snow is a sight of beauty that could not be compared. I know you would perhaps compare such beauty to my visage, but I also know that you lie, and I wish you would be able to lie to my face rather than through these written shapes and figures which are all meaningless without their author.

I read your letters and smell them despite their repugnant odor. I kiss the words between their lines. Sublime is the love I feel for a man so distant yet so nearby. Your words accompany me through the day, and in the night, I read them again, I have memorized them, I have memorized your handwriting and I could visualize the way your hand curves in writing every letter. Oh, how I could kiss these hands.

I know your landscape looks like a circle of hell but my hardship in waiting for your arrival has been testing my patience to its fullest. I tire in being accompanied by nothing but servants and echoing footsteps. I tire in waiting for you but I could see no way out. I am trapped as you are in your encampment but my confines are that of a mental space yet it feels all too real, like an invisible phantasm would shatter glass around the room. No one would believe you until they hear the noise and even then they would have doubts.

Tell me my dear, tell me about everything and know well that I do not fear losing a battle or even the entire war as long as I do not lose you. However, good news would not hurt, not one bit, if anything we need it for morale. Provisions are scarce but we will get through, they will last us until the end of winter. Maybe then, amongst the blossoming meadows, may we meet and kiss, may we forget the hard past and leave it well behind.

Yours,

Countess Claire of Calistero."

Constable Krill looked left and right in fear that he may be watched, affirming himself to being alone he closed his eyes and kissed the letter, holding it closely to his chest. As if in a brief state of trance, he reawakened and at once began writing his reply. Eleonore flew uncontrollably, making it hard for the constable to concentrate on his writings, but it was not her fault; she was being chased over and over by a savage cat who was Krill's favorite pet, after his horse, of course.

"Feckless feline!" exclaimed Eleonore.

"Flying rat!' exclaimed the cat.

"Why do you hunt me so? I'm on a mission. I know your kind. You sit on your hide all day while we fly for days delivering letters to your owners."

"Hah!" mocked Snowfluff, "I own him! Ask anyone at all and they would say the same. Oh, they would not dare claim otherwise, they would not dare!" The chase went on and on until the constable has had enough of the brat. He carried her, pinching her back neck, and kicked her out. Her final words as her tail left the room were, "I am related to the mighty Lion, the King of all..." Her meows went silent afterwards.

this fight, it is because of you, for the glory of your name and the banner of your ladyship, but above all the love I have for you.

The fervor in understanding the frailty of man and charging into battle makes my heart shiver, yet it beats in a rhythm tenfold in tempo upon seeing the bird with your letter attached, like a descent of a thing holier than heaven. You can only imagine my disappointment when the letter is not from you. We have fared well by luck thus far but lack shan't be always on our side and the tides of war may change to crush us soon. The cold is bearable yet the icy breeze that carries the stench of the rotten fallen from a mass open air sepulcher is an assault on every sense, and I am sorry it has been carried to you through my letters, a mistake I hope I have rectified with the perfume. We are engulfed by mud and blood and entombed by the snow, but God willing we shall endure. I have taken lifetime and again, and I shall do it again, if need be, but your words soothe my frenzy. I read them whilst taking care of life, I water my lilies or caress my cat, for all life is sacred and it is a reminder from God for us to take care of it. It seems humorous writing these words whilst I take more life come morn and yet I take care of these lesser beings. Perhaps it is the lack of speech or language of plants and animals that makes them loveable. Perhaps not.

Onto more pressing matters, your ladyship and I have been corresponding for long and I have been honest in every word I had written. But the words I have not said are lies, or perhaps redacted, left out willfully or...nay, they were left out willfully and not forgotten since I have thought to include them in every letter I have sent, yet I consciously leave them out. I would never lie about my love for you, but I did lie about my identity. I am not your husband; I have taken his position ever since he had fallen in battle a year ago. Sir Mortimer is a martyr or just another casualty I'm afraid, and we cannot retrieve his body for he has fallen in a place battle is still being done. This is a ferocious war in a scope unforeseen and by the end of it his body could be fully disintegrated.

I did not lie when I said that I loved you, I did not lie when I said that I would like to hold you in my arms. However, I did lie about my identity. As for my name, it is Krill. I have served as constable ever since your husband departed from this mortal coil. I was second in command, and I must say it was an honor serving under your husband. He was a good man, I'm sure you know this already.

I duly apologize,

Krill."

A secret confession was now a promulgation in the making. A public announcement brewing and waiting for the right audience to cause a proper scandal. As surely as the sky was blue, little by little, everyone knew, the rich, the poor, the beggarly, the young lovers who cheered for the blindness of love, and the married elderly who looked perturbed, making a mental image of the constable, painting him as an unfocused general whose mind was darkened by lusting over a woman he did not know and giving it priority over winning the war. The bard wrote a ballad recalling this incidence, a song forgotten in time:

> If I knew better
> and did not know,
> for love a letter
> with the wind that would blow.
>
> A man she loved,
> a man unknown,
> writ under a name
> not of his own.

A soldier was he
in a place far away.
She loved him still?
I cannot say.

No stranger was he,
oh no my dear!
He has written her
for more than a year

But I can sing,
for the blossoming spring,
and I could shout
about the encoded clout
delivered by a pigeon roaming about.

But I did not know
what truly happened,
The events as conspired
from beginning to end.

She loved him still?
Who could really say?
Nay, I could not talk ill
of the Countess in disarray.

He loved her or loved her not?
Only the petals could tell.
As for you, foolish lot,
you do not know her well.

She is a thing of majesty,
not only by name.
It would be a travesty
if by her lonesome she would remain.

But only time will tell, I say.
Only time will tell,
not you nor I could really say,
but we shall wish her well.

The weather, temperament, and beauty in her
was fair, and fair and fair.
I pray for the golden lock in her hair.
I pray for her well to fare.

The enjoyment of fiction overshadowed the truth. The events
have truly conspired and reality became myth. It was a cause of
clamor; a kerfuffle of noise and songs and thoughts about the
subject and somehow reality was lost. The names were changed.
Legends were born out of the tale, some included dragons and
warriors, others included paupers who turned to princes for they
loved royalty. The woman who truly knew what happened knew
not what to do. She sat in solitude, in a silence that would drive a
hermit mad. She demanded not to hear a single noise, but whispers
pursued, a faint volume reading her a tale behind her doors. A
hundred days and a hundred nights had passed since the scandal
and the Countess had recovered physically yet somewhere within
her psyche something was broken, even gone. She was played
like a fool, but she felt that beneath the burning emotions of a
woman betrayed, beneath the scintillating flame and fury of hatred
was the cognitive dissonance, the thought of also loving the man.
There was genuine emotions of compassion and care, and fear for

the anonymous man who sent her these letters. She gave it deep thoughts that took another hundred days and hundred nights of solitude. Finally, she made up her mind to know more about him before he too would fall in battle. She had to expect the worst for life was cruel and uncaring when men closed their hearts to all that's good in the world, such was the way of the warrior.

Eleonore had taken a well-deserved rest. She became idle for days on end and all she had done was sleep and eat and, at times, play with the local birds in the pond, bathing with them under the silver sky. It was a much-needed respite, not from her long travels but also from the emotional numbness of her lost youths and dead spouse. But the time for meditating was over for the Countess. She headed towards Eleonore. Deep thoughts have taken a toll on her. Her face has aged well in less than a year, Eleonore kissed her cheeks which put a smile on Claire's rosy face. She demanded her to go as fast as the winds would take her and not to tarry a second along the way. Off went Eleonore with newfound excitement for her journey, for she knew the destination and she knew the roads but every time something new came along, a new threat, a new enemy, or a new friend. She did not know and the only way she knew was to embark on the adventure and never cower from spreading her wings.

The constables' heart dropped, it skipped a beat, and then another. He would have died if not for the anticipation of reading the words within the sealed scroll descending with the bird. He had opened the seal and attentively went through the letter.

"Dear Constable Krill,

I have given this letter an amount of thought I have not given over any other matter in my entire lifetime, not even the time in which I reigned sovereign over my people, a timeline that lasted for more than a decade. I have taken this position of authority vowing

I would never fall into a tyrant's hands for fifteen years, ever since the age of eighteen in which I was taken up as a wife for my now fallen husband. Yet I have fallen for you, are you not a tyrant? Your actions must have had consequences that are grave in their nature, yet not only you walk free, but I crave you, and I want you to come to me, and only a tyrant walks free from crime. I hope you realize how much trouble you have been, you mischievous antagonist. An invisible man: a ghost who unsuspectingly stole a part of my heart. What do you look like, specter from afar? I demand to know. I could get any man in the kingdom to court me yet my heart desires this man of letters whose figure I can only imagine. Try to paint yourself with words, your height and stature and build, and try not to compliment yourself too much.

My emotions have swayed from grief over my lost husband, and elated joy in knowing the man with flowery words is alive and well. That is a relief, knowing there is still a man who cares for me not for my rank. I am self-aware how a woman who inhabits the upper echelon of society could be perceived, but I need kindness just the same, proper love that has been eclipsed in my life for far too long. It is time that hidden star has shone once again and this star burns for you, it burns because of you. It gladdens me to know the man who would care for me cares for flowers too, a thing so delicate and beautiful.

I have grown to be a lonely woman who could not bear her birthright of authority any longer. I did not ask for any of this in my life, yet it has been bestowed upon me by force. My husband made these burdens tolerable and, with him gone, the only thing that remains is my son, a relic of our love and the fruit of my own womb. He ignores me like the passing winds. His mind has been polluted ever since I have sent him to university where he learned, among the many subjects, to have delusions of grandeur and magnanimity.

In his last letter to me, he proclaimed that he did not want a mere throne, he wanted the entire world, if not to rule it with his own body, he would let his thoughts loose in every corner known to man. I still love him, he is my child after all, but he truly has gone mad, and I wait very patiently for him to calm down and come back home but he is ever so defiant. You men are a crucible, a cross for us to bear with your pride and your warmongering as if it were a game.

In short, I am left with you as the only man in my life, a man whom I have not met but know all too well. I never have pleaded or begged in my life, but I beg you not to leave me.

I pray this war will be over, for your sake, your mother's sake, and for my sake.

Above all, for my sake. Such a proclamation is not selfish. I need you.

Yours, as you are mine,

Claire."

The constable whose heart started beating like a stampede of wild animals whilst reading this letter with fear of rejection and reproach was now calm. His melting waxen heart remolded with her words. He closed his eyes and imagined holding the lady herself between his arms rather than the letter. At once, he began to write a response.

"Madame Countess,

An old man once said, "only the dead have seen the end of war," perhaps it's true, I do not wish to come back to your castle as carrion carried on a wheelbarrow. I want to walk to you, no matter the distance, I shall march far and long until I reach you. If I survive onslaught after onslaught of rabid men, I shall walk to you. That is my promise, to live and to die on my feet, standing firm and standing tall. It is exhausting, marching from place to place, leaving in our wake death and destruction. This time I shall march for your love once this battle is over, that is. I assure you, my flowers blossom still, but with certainty I say you shall be the finest flower I have ever taken care of in my life.

As for your son, the ne'er do well, he would do better if he unlearnt his pettiness and learnt some humility. Too bad without the teachings of God, such a virtue has no use in our world. He must know that outside of a mother's touch, outside of a mother's womb, all notions of love are those of convenience and utility; how useful a man is to his wife or lover is a construct so frail when brought to question and tampered by the fire of life and the trials it has to offer. Only a woman would embrace her child in the magma of this hellscape. Life is suffering my dear; to live is to suffer, and I only wish my mother were alive to hold me. Her arms would not wrap around me as well for her bones were not as flexible and elastic and my shoulders have grown significantly in width. But alas, it does not matter, for I would not caress a skeleton.

I wish you would not judge us men too harshly, for pride gets the best of us oftentimes, and we need to remember that in history, pagan emperors ruled as gods. Perhaps men have not outgrown that phase of wanton glory knowing well that it has been trumped by our lord and savior, Jesus Christ, hallowed be his name. The rest of us mortals are nothingness embodied in ashen sculptures that will turn to dust in no time. Nothing is guaranteed in life but death.

Enough with my nihilistic drivel. Let me describe myself. I am a man of a handsome visage. My skin is white in winter and red in the summer. I have brown hair and a well shaven face. My eyes are blue, and my nose is small. As for my stature, I am not so tall. My muscles are well formed, no doubt from the constant battle in which I engage and will engage in come tomorrow and the day after. King Edward is a tyrant whose reign will come in my lifetime, preferably by my own hands.

Whatever happens, I promise to see you soon.
Yours and yours alone,
Krill."

Krill called the marshal to send the pigeon on its way with the letter and instantly started planning for an attack.

"At this hour of day sir?" asked the marshal.

"I have pressing matters to attend to, and yes dear friend, now is the time to strike."

The marshal smiled and was more than happy to oblige. They rounded up the men and marched under the moonlight glow, a night whose blackness was stripped away by a moon so close and grand.

Eleonore went back and forth, back and forth, until she had collapsed from exhaustion in the middle of nowhere, as if camouflaged in the white snow a figure emerged, its symmetry once disappearing now shaped a cat. Was it a ghost or was it real? Either way, it had given the bird sufficient reason to fear, but she could not move, the poor thing, her stiffness from the cold preceded that from terror. She watched helplessly, her eyes drunk with prayer, captain Snowfluff drew near. A silent encounter it was at first before the silence was broken with a question.

"Do you not want to eat me?"

"Why you silly thing, I just wanted to play! But enough about that, shush now," Snowfluff provided the helpless bird with shelter beneath his thick fur coat. He placed the poor shivering bird beneath his body and lay on it, her head beneath his face was left exposed to breathe in the cold air.

"Why are you not in the tent? Why are you so far away from the camp? Would not the constable be scared for your fate?" question after question she asked, perhaps in fear still of the beastly Maine Coon.

The cat closed its eyes. Part melancholic, part exhausted, "I said shush," he concluded all dialogue for the night.

Dusk came along and with it the faintest rays of light descended upon all things living and dead. The mist made it hard to fly and even harder to see, but Eleonore had places to be. One place in particular now. She looked around and all she saw was the omnipresent morning dew, asides from the cats footprints there was no trace of him. The footprints like little pins caving in the ground, drowning in this new layer of earth. The bird flew, barely taking off the ground, but she did not cease until she reached her destination. There, upon seeing the faulty way she flew, the constable put her in a cage with a small pillow, there she lay for long.

"The bird suffers. I shan't let her leave before the sun shines, nor would I allow it to come back in such a condition," he said in silent monologue. He took pity on her state and pet the little bird, "one more voyage my dear, the final one."

In the castle most august, silent hums of joy played like an instrument in the Countess' cavernous chamber. She danced behind closed doors as passersby from servants to family wondered what was happening. Her mother walked in without knocking with a tea tray in her hand.

"Mother!" exclaimed Claire to the woman who barged in, taking a good look at her as she seemed of a perfect fit. Yes indeed, she was short but not too short.

"Why do you look at me so, child? I have brought you tea if you should drink with me." She entered, putting down her tray at a circular wooden table in the middle of the room, her daughters' bright, smiling eyes chased her observantly. Without a word uttered, she grabbed her mother, as shocked as she was, the old woman turned then grabbed her daughter's hands. They danced and danced around and around the table.

In the tent, the constable danced on his lonesome, both hands above him, the right one in front of his face, her hips would be held that way if she was as tall as they said she was, and his left hand stretching to the heavens, grabbing nothing.

The marshal came in with urgent news. The constable's eyes shone. He was dumbfounded in the sudden entrance, everyone knew better than to interrupt, especially when uninvited and with nothing to report, not that he let the poor man speak.

"Get out! No wait, come in, come in!" capricious were his demands.

"Sir?" the marshal peaked his head in as if her had not intruded already.

"Come hither," the constable demanded, and the marshal obliged.

"Closer," he took a short step forward in the tent.

"Damnit lad, come and dance!"

"But sir! It's hardly appropriate."

"It's not for you, you fool, it's for the Countess. We are on good terms now. Better than good I dare say. So good I anticipate taking her up as a wife upon arrival."

"That is good news, sir," the marshal locked into dance with the constable.

"Right. Now, firm your hips. Good. Raise your head man, stop looking down at me, its condescending!" They danced in the hopes that no one saw them with frequent glances to the door. But Eleonore saw and laughed from afar. The marshal reported that the advancement they had done at night was to their advantage; they had the upper hand on the unsuspecting enemies, possibly marking the end of the battle if they agreed to surrender. The warrior smiled. It was time for his final message, it was time for his final blow.

"It takes the bird seven days to get to the Countess, yes?"

"Yessir."

"Then, we have seven days to march to her."

"Impossible! What about the cold? What about the horses? Who shall take care of them?"

"They shall come with us, and you shall only ride on horseback. I will walk."

"Are you going to walk all the way?"

"All the way indeed."

The marshal looked at his superior in disbelief, but he had seen his mad ambitions come to fruition. He took unimaginable risks and yet he had delivered his troops to the bays of victory time and again. He nodded, attached the last letter to Eleonore, and left the tent as the bird flew.

The sun rose seven times, and so did the moon as she waited for a promised letter from her windowpane. The moonlight was split by the cedar tree adjacent to her window. She sat with her head nestled between her hands in the dark spot. Before her slumberous eyelids would fall, she beheld the letter descending. "Open the gates," it read. From the horizon, she could see a hazy collection of heads like marching ants. They were not too many, maybe a couple of dozen men. They came closer and closer still. She could not contain her excitement. She did not care at that instance how the man looked like. She rushed to welcome him brushing past many as if she saw nothing other than the marching men. She reached the gates and demanded they were open at once. Claire was happy to see the man approach, even happier seeing he did not exaggerate, his handsomeness was understated and his stature not as short as she expected. He kept his promise, a tribute of love. He did march to her, the sweat on his brow dropped to his toes, his weapons and armor soaked in blood, and in his hand a vase in which a flower rested in water and a note attached to it, it reads, "If one loves a flower, he would leave it untouched, but none has loved as much as I, and if it mean the flower has to die, I would at once sacrifice it at our altar. Saint Valentine have mercy on us." A shower of embraces and kisses over the muck-painted warrior besmirched with the foulness of war, he looked at her face, it was radiant with joy, a smile whose curve was carved in marble, in unfaltering joy. Her white skin and green eyes were a sight he longed for in a dream. He chased behind her in nightmares in which a figure he imagined to be her was walking away, but there she was, and he had nothing to say. Without a word, he kissed her hand. They feasted and sang and danced throughout the night and day. Despite his exhaustion, he awakened himself time and again to see her next to him. There was no reason to sleep and fall into the arms of a dream as long as she was near. Arm in arm, he went to battle with his comrades, and arm in arm, he celebrated with his love. He thanked God for not leaving him on his own for a moment in his life. He reported to her after a long night of festivities when the crowds went silent from the languor of drunkenness and a prolonged dancing.

"Milady, we have escaped the jaws of death and malady in your ladyships name. We emerge victorious from the villains of the tyrant, as you are aware by now that we have turned against the King as he has turned against himself. I am afraid we have lost many good men in the process." He took a moment of silence to pay respect to the dead, "we shall borrow some wheelbarrows and horses to retrieve them, with your permission of course."

"You have it, without question. They shall embark whenever you order them to."

"We are all yours, milady, the horses, the troops." He looked into her eyes as if taking permission yet simultaneously demanding to kiss her lips, "above all, I am yours." The people hailed the constable and his troops. One last loving look he sent her before he collapsed in her bosom. He could not revive himself from the final sleeping spell. The next day he awakened, showered in pleasant congenial odors, they had no doubt bathed him whilst unconscious. He lifelessly stared at the wooden roof; he could not believe the streak of good luck that had recently come his way. He had heard and sent tales of tragedy and horror for the families of the fallen for years and years, to the point that knowing death awaited him did not matter. He was desensitized and detached to the tragedy of inexistence. He was certain he would never wake up, that one day everything will go dark, and he will hear nothing, see nothing, and be nothing. But there he was, and with her in his arms, everything outside of her bedroom did not matter. He kissed her sleeping face and in serendipitous stupor, he closed his eyes again.

Eleonore went back to her cage within the walls of Vorwahl, seeing love bloom like springtime in the barren cold brought her back to life and back to living. She, of course, did not forget the blessed dead for they remained within her, head, and heart and all. Settling in, once again, she grew closer and closer to the stranger in the pen. He would dance a little mating dance after a week of knowing her, and after a month of flying around together, they have decided to take their relationship a step forward. Shaw and Sue were to depart for good. They approached Melvin in the night as every living thing in the castle, except for a few breathing flowers, was in deep slumber.

"Melvin, we are leaving," Shaw informed him as he opened his eyes, "possibly for good."

"Why you two lovebirds, of course!" Melvin scared himself awake with the high-pitched exclamation. He paused to see if he had awakened anyone near him, "of course, depart at once. You deserve the best. Are you going to serve the Countess or are you going feral?"

"We have not decided yet," Eleonore said, with her head caressing Shaw's, "but we shall be together, no matter what happens."

Melving cooed his excitement. He was at loss for words, "Go now, leave! Goddess be with you."

"Is it not better to inform the others?" both asked concerned about the others might say.

"Absolutely not, why would you subject yourself to their shallow rumors and empty words. No, no, depart in the peaceful night, out of mind and out of sight," Melvin embraced them both and with great joy witnessed their departure, in the hopes he would hear from them again. Whatever happens, he knew that love would guide them. He was left in the darkness pondering upon his youth and the days he flew freely with his wife.

Chapter Five

SLAVE FOR THE PAST

"You knights are quite the bastards," said the free woman, the maiden concealed in white, still wearing the knights' coat.

"How so, milady?" asked Sir Sebastian. The cold was starting to penetrate his skin, but he would forbear from complaints for they were almost out of the bounds of winter in a land far away. He could take his coat, but he would not allow the maiden to suffer on his behalf.

"You walk with royalty and the destitute alike and are welcomed by both with a cordiality fit for royal blood. You live with both, but for whom would you die? I wonder if it is fear from your expertise in butchering that grants you all this love."

"I assure you; you have nothing to fear. I have time to spare, and I would gladly guide you to safety."

"Lucky, lucky me. Am I to you what a harlequin is to a king? A pleasant way to make time pass."

"It's not that. It's in our code of honor to save helpless maidens."

"Hah. 'Code of honor', I'll believe it when I see it my dear. And rest assured, I can fight for myself. It's the mere fact that I am not accustomed to such cold nor am I prepared for it, that was the reason for my brief falling in captivity."

"May I ask what you were doing near the castle? I have heard rumors you took part in besieging it."

"Me? Oh no, look at these feeble arms, I wouldn't hurt an insect even if I tried."

"One moment you are mighty, another you are feeble. You confuse me."

She smiled, riding her captors' horse with the knight walking by her side. They took turns in riding the beast for she refused to be touched by him. "Now that you have saved your 'damsel in distress,' you can go now. I'm sure you have many lovers awaiting."

"I'm afraid no one awaits me outside the killing field." Her compliments did not go unnoticed, but he had a force of habit in being laconic. They have threaded for days on the silent ground, asides from the birds and the thick-skinned or furred animals, there was no sign of life. There were green pine trees, cedars trees, oaks, and naked olive trees, and all were dancing to the silent in-cantation of a winters spell. They breathed the cold winters scent, and as they passed by them, they swore they heard them, as if they gained sudden sentience, speaking of their love. They have grown accustomed to one another. There was a semblance of something akin to romance in the tense air between them, charged with pri-mal instincts and teasing tributes. They grew closer in heart and mind but physically he kept his distance, that was until she let him ride on the horse with her. He could not act upon his emotions, nor would he take initiative knowing what he knew, doing what he had done. Perhaps, he wondered, perhaps she was not the woman he thought she was. He pleaded she be straight with him until he got his answer. They grew closer, close enough to know more intimate details of one another.

"I have a name, you know."

"Milady?"

"No, it's not 'Milady', it's Margaret."

"Margaret, lovely name for a person lovelier still. My name is…"

"Sir Sebastian," she cut him off, "how could I forget, the moment you rescued you identified yourself," she copied in mocking mimicry his very motion at the time. She put her hand on her breast and puffed, thickening her voice, "My name is Sir Sebastian and I have come to rescue you."

He let out a brief laughter, "You see, I must identify myself, it is in our code for us to scream our names in case any witnesses saw our bravery they would have the correct names. But my name does not matter next to a rose as beautiful as thee, all that matters is your safety." She blushed and wondered why he sat silence when she was trying to familiarize herself with him. It was a silent travel from there on after.

They have reached her humble abode and there she confessed, "since we're far away and I have the entire town to fight back with me in case you decide to take me back to be judged by your criminals. Yes, I was a mercenary, and I took my son and buried him there. I thought he could fight, and for his age he was brave and strong beyond comparison." There was a change in her emotions from playfulness to a far graver posture, "I was a fool. I thought we could make money, enough gold to survive not just the winter, but seasons on end. We could have anything to eat or drink at our whims delight, to have what we please and when we please it. I wanted to replace my hut and build a new one, or maybe even own a mansion befit for kings, with stables, horses, cows, and all forms of cattle with a stretch of farmland as far as the eye could see. One would be foolish to call this greed; it is not greed if it is ambition, I just want enough for me without taking from another, something royalty would never understand."

The knight stood as motionless and as lifeless as a sculpture of a man; after her affirmation of his doubts, it was now his turn to concede to his wrongdoings. He reached for his hilt, as soon as his hand reached his waist. At once, she was alarmed and carried her knife with a deathly grip, the sharp end pointing to the man. There was a safe distance between them and while she considered him as a threat. He was at that moment his worst enemy for his lips would not move which made him seem as if preparing for combat. With a tremor he confessed, "I have slain your son." Falling, he knelt and gave up his sword to the ground, "I am sorry..."

"Don't you dare," roared the sky. She conducted the horrible cacophony and the earth itself shook with a command from her mouth, then came the sudden awkward silence in which she held back tears. She could not. She could explode into pathetic sobs there. She stood biting her lips, her eyes two protruding rubies in inexpressible rage and sorrow. She waited, willing to humor whatever words he may stumble upon in his mind, knowing well within forgiveness was out of the question.

"You may kill me where I stand, alternatively, I offer myself as a slave. You may whip me, you may force me to work all day and all night, you may imprison me for as long as you wish." He kept his eyes fixated to the ground. He did not need to look at her to know how she wept or how bitter were her tears and vicious her gaze in looking at the perpetrator, the merchant of her misery.

"Very well," she choked on her words, foaming one last command, "crawl."

He tried to raise his head to see where he was to go but she would not let him, she would strike him down to the ground every time he tried to get up until he understood the gravity of the situation. He did indeed crawl to his room, a few steps on his heels took an eternity on his belly. He had shallow wounds, the skin on his bones was torn by the sharp flints and edged pebbles on the road. He was tied to a rope, despite his promises of not leaving, and left to sleep on the ground. Her movement was automatic, as if she could not hear nor see nor think properly. She went to another room in a corner of the small house where her tears were without cessation and her wails without bounds, breaking physical barriers of wood and stone to reach many neighbors, some of whom witnessed firsthand all that had happened in repudiation ever since her arrival with the strange man.

Chapter Six

THE GOD OF
THIS WORLD

The torturer rose in his dingy, dark excuse of a room, and it was, by all means, a room; four straight perpendicular walls held the ceiling up high above his head, but that was it. He had no window from which light would shine, nor did he have a bed to sleep on. At times, it seemed he punished himself as equally as he had punished others. He had no memory of a smile. All that accompanied him in his chambers were bellowing shrieks of broken men, and very infrequently, an unfortunate woman would fall in his hands. For as long as he could remember, that was what he did, as if nothing came before and nothing will come after. The priest was a problem. He had promised to do two things to him; one was to keep him safe from harm and the other to kill him and deliver his body to his companions. How could he do both? That was all he thought of day and night, a sleep depriving enigma that had no obvious answer. The pigeons came and left, day in and day out with a message on their chests, "where is the body, Tobias? Don't you dare break the promise. Such an action will have grave consequences." He thought about reporting them to the King, but they were his associates, they were untouchable as long as they had obeyed the old man. Another uncomplicated solution would have been to flee, but the King had eyes for as far and as wide as the known world, and they were loyal to him as long as his kingdom prevailed.

In his hands, there was the end of a long rope of gold. He had sent both bags of coins he had been paid to the jeweler for him to make it. At the end of it, he had made a noose which he put around his neck for so long he had forgotten about its weight hugging his upper spine. In a silent lament, these words formed in his head, "if only I had thought about this before. I could still kill the priest." He thought about it through and through, but he had never broken a promise, and even if he was accused of greed to the point of avarice, he was still a man of principle and once a payment had reached his pockets, a deal was sealed. He called to his brother, the nameless executioner. In his ravenous bloodthirst, his brother was hardly human, but even the most mindless and savage of animals would respect their siblings to a certain degree. He was large in mass, like a boulder of stone, of fat and muscle hiding his bones. "Listen, I might have to leave to the most dangerous of lands known to man. You shall take my place for as long as I am absent. For the love of God, do not kill anyone." These were not suggestions, they were orders, even if the brother exceeded the torturer in mass, he feared him as a younger brother would naturally fear his elder. It was only natural that there might have been a touch of reverence for him, but in their lines of duty, there was no such thing as reverence, love, or care. There was only respect, and it was a result of fear.

Tobias rode in a dead night. Asides from his torch, there was no light in sight. No one to see or hear what he was up and about to do in this hour of day. The moon hid in the infinite colorless firmament above, the silence was interrupted only by the hooting of owls which accompanied him, the ever-watching eyes of the birds of prey were no threat to him, nor were they friendly. They merely existed. The acrid stench closing in, in its intensity he could taste his nausea, this has marked his arrival to the place he wanted to be. Dismounting his horse, he heard a voice call out to someone, in a jerky motion he tried to hide himself, but he was exposed. Even if he threw his torch aground, he could not evade the memory of the strangers. There were trees here, the trunks blasphemously called out the rest of their bodies in pain, just like the fallen men had done before, the jagged edges of the cuts implied they were not cut but dismantled by cannonballs. The blackened soil muddied with sanguineous sleep; eternal slumber they had been granted. Dead upon dead, they laid in positions that did not seem comfortable, not even to him. All that remained was torrential rain and downpour on the centennial eve of war. The earth dampened, mudded by water from heaven and the blood of the fallen, his impeded motion came to an absolute stop.

"Halt! Thieving scum."

"I am no thief, Sir! I am on monarchial mission!"

"From which king? Speak before an arrow strikes your neck."

"King Ed...Julian, Sir. Julian." Tobias noticed their banner, it looked like a thorned rose from afar meaning they did not serve Edward but rather his enemy.

"Lies. Show us your permit." Tobias was relieved that his guess was right.

"No permit, Sir, I am directly related to his majesty."

"No permit means no passage, graverobber. Turn back to where you came from and cause no further disturbance," demanded the guard overlooking the operation of cleaning up the bodies, sending individual cadavers one after another to their families. In the usual battle, in a scale as grand as this, the bodies were left to rot or consumed by scavengers or vultures, but the constable gave the people a promise upon his return and had kept it, and so did the torturer; he was not going to leave with empty hands. He concealed himself in twigs and leaves of the dead trees and waited. The men worked all night long and it was only a matter of time before they were tired to the point of fatigue, some weaker willed individuals were bound to collapse. Unsurprisingly, a man had fallen asleep away from the torches of the other hard workers. The torturer with droopy eyes crept towards him, stole his clothes, and turned back to look at the dormant man. Was he to be a threat once awake? Should he kill him while he sleeps to forestall any further interruptions? His plan went seamlessly, but he was half asleep himself now; his limbs were debilitated with the encumberment of the consciousness which awakened past its bedtime. "No", he said to himself. He would see this through till the end without bloodshed.

The people were dulled with exhaustion to question those who threaded upon these forbidden grounds, who had permits or who did not. Like an automated machine, their limbs moved without thoughts, and their thoughts waned without warning to a dreamlike state of hypnosis, a somnambulance so trance like one would say they were enchanted by an invisible spirit, a witch, or a magical spell of some sort. He took advantage of that and hurried as he could to get his hands on a wheelbarrow. He held his eyelids in between his index fingers and middle fingers to watch closely the shapes of the bodies, on the surface the frozen yet torched figures were partially cremated. He could only imagine the pain went through, but realistically, he could not. Deep in the pit, there was one not too different from Jeremiah; the resemblance was not uncanny but there was sufficient likeness to catch his attention. His senses were dulled from the constant inhalation of the scent of death and the sights of human savagery. He had to leave as soon as possible to preserve what little sanity left within. He grabbed the intact body; it was warm in comparison to other bodies he had removed from atop of it. "Strange," he wondered to himself, maybe the layers of flesh above kept it at a reasonable temperature. He did not and could not give it more thought for his energies were waning, they were adequate for merely one task and that was the task at hand. He put the body in a wheelbarrow and made way to his horse. Before he could reach his steed, an appalling skeleton of a man was dancing as if he was trying to hover above the earth as his bare feet barely caressed the cold snow with every retracting step. He screamed in panic some unintelligible vituperations to the machinated men. At once, everyone had awakened from their spell; all faces could be recognized except the one in the dark, for he had to be the intruder, he had to be killed. Dread descended upon him, he was now physically encumbered by nothingness. His mind broke and frazzled. The feverish hectic thoughts were acted upon in a crawling speed, he tried again and again to attach the wheelbarrow to his horse as the first arrow missed his head by an inch, he then could function normally, it was his wake-up call. The wheelbarrow was now attached, and Tobias rode his horse as fast as he could, miraculously missed by his enemy's shots one after another. The sleepwalking horse riders could not hit him even if their lives depended on it.

Clear from hostile eyes, Tobias headed to the prison. He shaved the body's head in a way resembling the priest's, that is a tonsure, he then cleaned it from the filth it had accumulated, all that was left was the task of dressing it appropriately. He went down to the priests' cell to see him awake in an hour of day where all life lay asleep.

"I need your robe, friend." demanded Tobias, "I got you something else to keep you warm, even warmer than before."

The priest was flabbergasted by his change of heart, "one day you were flaying my skin off, the next you're keeping me warm. To what do I owe this pleasure?" inquired he in a geniune tone that was not demanding nor bitter.

"Whatever I say, you're going to thank God anyway. Please, take off your robe, it just might save your life." Without further questions, the priest took off his clothes and put on a much warmer attire; it was made out of bear skin, the warmth at once set in, as if he had suddenly escaped winter within his walls.

It was a nocturnal affair, the returning of the departed. With dusk struggling to cast the earth's sleepy ever-watching single eye of the sun, the first rays of light were struggling to descend from the heavens beneath the clouds above. The torturer thought this was the perfect opportunity to set off to the monastery, chance and circumstance were on his side, and in the darkness what little features that may seem different at first glance will be overlooked, or at least he thought they would be and thus, he set out on his journey with the body in the wheelbarrow. Upon arrival, he knocked on their doors and beheld for a silent moment the starry firmament as best as he could as it were hidden above the opaque pre-morning dew.

The doors opened. Before being greeted by the brown robed men, the odorous vapors of their succulent-looking meals reached his nostrils. There was buttered turkey with garlic and basil, roasted to a golden-brown perfection. They drank fresh milk with cinnamon and honey. There were many different kinds of quality brews, be it ale or beer, sweet breads and savory doughs, fresh fruits past their seasons of harvest made their way to the table alongside dairy based desserts and a multitude of cakes, and many other delicious meals whose vapors rose in the cold air had driven him to walk inside without welcome and a priest whispered to another as he passed the gravy, "...and after all, man shall not live on bread alone." Tobias slobbered over the delights set upon the table. His diet was that of peasantry; fish and bread and a bit of wine or beer, seeing what he saw he thought it to be no wonder that the lot were obese, such sights would tempt a fasting hermit with a will of iron. As they were distracted in feasting, he extinguished the flames of as many candles as he could without being noticed, and then he stood, clearing his throat for the big announcement.

"Behold, the man you have asked for, in the flesh, decayed as it is. He is within your grasp at last. Now, come and see," his hands pointed in true showmanship fashion to the wheelbarrow. There he was the lifeless doppelganger laid asleep on hard wood and splinters. There were gasps and awes and many other reactions, disgust at the sight of death next to those of delight, not that it would obstruct their rapacious appetite. Many things were said, shouted even, but none were intelligible. In the midst of chaos and noise, he could see the body open its eyes wide open. At once and without much thought, he closed his hand into a firm fist and hit him as hard as he could on the back of the skull.

"My dear torturer, your work here is done! We know that you are vigorous and single-minded, but you have tortured the man to the point of death, I think that would be enough," spoke Cecil in sarcasm.

"We shall see about that." Upon saying those words, Tobias took the body before the priests could object, before their throats could swallow what food they masticated in massive mouthfuls and hurried to the prison. Was it possible that they did not see this abomination? This Lazarus like miracle that could have landed him in a heap of trouble that had a beginning but no end. It didn't matter, for he was far away from them now.

From a safe distance under a fiery pearl of a sun whose earliest rays raced down to the earth, they reflected on the muddied snow and made everything brighter. Tobias sat at the side of a frozen pond, its crystal-clear mirror surface reflected the face that gazed upon it, beneath the slender icy surface, beneath the blue sky the fish swam as if they flew and as clueless as if they knew. The torturer looked at his reflection. He then saw the fish travelling around his head. As he was lost in thought, mystified in the perplexity of what to do, there was noise. Before he could turn around, the body had arisen from the wooden structure and pushed the man. He stumbled to the ground, sliding into a distance far from the edge.

"My head still hurts, you imbecile," the dead man spoke.

"You're supposed to be dead!" exclaimed Tobias, who laid with his belly hugging the cold in fear of straying further. His bedazzled eyes gazed into the blinding light of the pond in the hopes and in prayer that the ice won't break beneath his weight.

"That...that is a mistake on my part. Well, I would help you if I could lad, but you're too far away now."

"Wait," he begged of him. The end of the rope around his neck was now in his right hand and he promptly threw it to the stranger. "Here, I beg you to drag me to solid land, I will be greatly indebted to you."

The undead soldier looked at the rope and, without much thought, held it in his hand and took one step backwards after another. Tobias thanked heaven and realized the fault in his ways; the rope that was to take his life has saved him by a man he pulled from a grave. This strange string of events had made him believe in divine providence if only for a second. It was then he realized only the desperate look for signs. He removed the noose and thanked the stranger with a croaky voice from a recovering throat.

"Would you mind explaining to me what on earth is happening?"

"You would not understand," the nameless man said, "You would not understand. One way to man's head would be reason, but reason is limited to what is known, the other is the senses, in seeing what is shown. Come with me, come, and see for yourself." Without a word further, the man walked. Tobias was calming his nerves until he saw the distance the stranger drew from him; it was then that he detached the wheelbarrow from the horse and walked with the stranger.

"You know, I have a question myself," asked the stranger, "what is it that wrapped your neck?"

The torturer smiled and passed it above his head and unto the horse's saddle, "That, my friend, is the wealth I have amassed. Much good it did me."

Chapter Seven

OF PIGEONS
AND MEN

The pigeons came and left the caretakers quarter with a simple horribly written letter, "sned more." Again and again, the content of the letter would change at times from "sned moer" to "sden mroe" to "sedn roem." It was gibberish and the sender was anonymous. It was taken at first as a lighthearted joke but then it became vexatious. All enjoyment had ceased when this red-sealed letter was opened by the King for him to read two gibberish words. This nuisance of a man would not cease from sending these pigeons to and from the royal quarter, and the King could not let Francis open red-sealed letters unattended. His patience had grown thin until he snapped. He sent letters to the sender whose whereabouts were unknown to him; only the pigeons knew where he resided. The last pigeon to go there was Susan. She did not stop mourning her child ever since he had fallen in the trials, but her work was like an impulse as natural as eating and sleeping. There was no pressure for her to do it. She was more than happy to be on her merry way. Francis attached a letter to her in one sunny day and without a word she left her recovering daughter with her husband. Below her, she witnessed the royal guard following; their eyes set skyward as they marched onwards. They tripped and fell over their horses many times clashing into oncoming traffic as well as rocks and trees, as humorous as it were to witness it from above, she knew it was an ominous sign for the recipient. Charles descended from his chariot; he was disoriented from the horrible driving, intoxicated with rage knowing he had reached the prankster in person. He waited to see him carry the pigeon, he seemed to disregard the letter and directly attach a new one.

"Halt!" he demanded. The simple man dropped the bird from his hands.

"You scare me sir! how may I help you?"

"I am his majesty's advisor." At once, the simple man bowed in front of his dilapidated, single roomed house.

"At your service, Sir."

"Do not play the part of the fool, you imbecile. Stop sending useless mail. This is your last warning."

"It's not useless, Sir. We need help, I have heard that pigeons help. See, my wife is barren."

"And the pigeons would help how?"

"A friend of mine has told me one of them might descend with a baby one day. See, my wife is barren, she has been infertile no matter how hard we tried to get a baby. That is why I have urged you to send us more. I have memorized how to write these two words and…"

"You have never written it proper. It reads send more, you imbecile," he spelled it out for him, "S. E. N. D. M. O. R. E."

"Then send more, Sir, send more!"

"No!" the advisor growled at the insolence, "this is the last bird you will get from his majesty; you will trouble him no more. and this letter is your last warning."

"But I don't know how to read, Sir."

"You don't have to, just keep in mind this piece of paper next time you think about sending the King a message. Do not obstruct royal duties any further. Understood?"

He looked at the ground, speechless in disappointment, as if a part of him has died, as if he was promised salvation and salvation itself has come to tell him there is none.

"I need to hear it from you, I need to know that you will not send us again."

"Understood. My last letter is already within your possession."

"Good." He said this last word menacingly, he was a shadow after all, he did not belong to the sun. It had bought him great discomfort to go outside, so much that he had forgotten to ask the man about how he had possessed red wax.

With his head stooping below his shoulder blades, the man carried the pigeon inside with him in great dismay.

"No use, my love. They won't send us the pigeons we need."

"Pigeons?" asked his wife, "You must ask for storks, you fool!"

"Why does it matter, woman?"

"A baby would easily fit a stork's mouth, on the other hand, how would a pigeon carry a baby. Silly, silly man."

"Oh!" exclaimed the simple man, this sudden realization descended upon him like a revelation. But his simplicity was not all bad, it had saved him from certain death while coming face to face with the advisor. "Oh well," he lamented, "it is too late now, far too late. We shall abate from sending letters to the King. What shall we do with the little bird?"

"Do what you will with it," she turned around in her side of the bed uncaringly, shutting her sad eyes to sleep.

The man looked at the bird and put her down, leaving her to her own devices. She could leave whenever she would like to, but she did not. Susan watched from the bottom rail of the bed, beneath their feet. She witnessed what they would do, and they would not do much other than snivel and growl with their fists pointing to the roof, or perhaps the cosmos above; they were in great anger and agitation, nothing would bring them peace. Susan wondered what the reason for that was. At the darkest hour of night, when they have gone to sleep and the candles were extinguished, she had looked for clues to tell her about the couple. She was supposed to be asleep herself, but curiosity had had the best of her. She grabbed previous letters they have received from the constable and read them fast in order not to get caught. She then realized, reading letter after letter that the couple's son had fallen in battle after fighting with great bravery. This fact had reminded her of her own tragedy. She could sympathize with the couple, for she had felt the same gushing feelings of hatred, distress, and despair. There was nothing she could do; she went back inside and locked the door.

Days passed, and nothing would happen. The couple did not move from their beds. They have slumbered for days, fasting from food, and only forcefully hydrating themselves every passing day from a jug of pottery that Susan had filled every now and then from a nearby well without them noticing. They have not eaten a thing for a week. Their shapes were starting to attenuate. Their limbs have become needle-like, and their bellies constricted. Their ribs have become boney, and their faces skull shaped. Their cheeks sunk, and the rest of the facial features exaggerated. Susan watched helplessly as the events unfolded. She hurried to the couple's cattle held up in the tithe barn for help.

"May I have a moment of your time?" She had gathered the cows, the pigs, and the hens all around in a circle. "Your owners torture themselves in sorrow, we need to help them."

"Oh, but I like Mr. and Ms. Mime, they were always good to us," said the cows.

"Always," replied the hens.

"Always, indeed," said the pigs.

"Very well, then you have ample reason to rescue them," demanded Susan.

"Now that you mention it," said the cows, "it is true they have left us enough food and water for a week, but they have not come to see us in a long time." The other animals agreed. The chickens glided from the windows of the tithe barns. The cows and pigs came to work together in breaking down the doors. Splinters, nails, and chains came flying about like an explosion. Thundering sounds had awakened the priests above who were watching guard from their monastery. The animals then swiftly made their way to the couple's home, once there and before any warning they broke down the doors.

"Why have you done that?" asked Susan, "I could have opened the door myself you know."

"It's fine," responded the pig, "if they have truly been asleep for a week, they need some shocking event to wake them up properly." Two figures dressed in brown were looming in from afar. The simple man awakened, stupefied in seeing the livestock come to him. His wife lifted her lifeless eyes to see the animals gathered at her doorstep and, without much thought, she scolded her husband, "you have not fed them, have you? Goodness me, can't you do anything properly?" Of course, this was a rhetorical question, but the man answered anyways, "but I did, I promise I did." His strength had been drained from the narcoleptic despondency which did not help in relieving him from the disconsolate reality, but the presence of the animals which was soon followed by the priests have shaken him to his core in the urgency of the sudden matters at hand, his sentimental state did not matter now, he had to answer to authority.

"What's this then?" asked Cecil, with Felix by his side who stood as motionless and as speechless as stone.

"I swear it is not what it seems, I have not smuggled these animals, nor did I call for them."

"I saw them escape by their own devices; I wonder why but it does not matter. Someone must pay for the damage done," Cecil demanded.

"I have lost my door too," pointed the farmer to the empty gap between the walls where his door once stood, "I suffer from this animalistic rampage as well as you."

"Am I my brothers' keeper?" said the priest, "my dear fallen son of Eve, it is not my problem what happens to you personally, personal problems must be solved by the individual himself. But you see, the tithe barn is communal, and you have taken care for all these brainless beasts, you are to be held accountable. I expect new doors to be erected by the end of the day."

"But Sir..." The argument was interrupted.

"By nightfall, kind Sir. It is enough time, I'm sure." Before another word could be spoken, the couple have turned their backs and taken strides away from the doorless house and the horrendous smell of the unbathed animals. Mr. Mime stood silently. His slender figure could barely hold him upwards without fatigue, for he was thin even before he had fasted for days and nights on end. He had to break his fast; the hens laid eggs for him, and the cows were ready to be milked. Worry had set in on him before he broke his fast. His tongue had yearned to taste anything at all, even though his breakfast was simple, it was beyond delicious, an ambrosial aroma emanated from it overshadowing the smells that were ejected from the animals. A few moments of silence followed, the trees shook off the dew from their branches from a breeze as gentle as a lover's caress, the birds sang a merry little song, then Susan spoke, "what now?"

"I am the one who is supposed to ask you this question," answered Mr. Mime.

"You speak to us sir?" asked the pig.

"There is no one else around," said the man, "I have been speaking to you for years and yet you ignore my words like the passing wind."

"We did not know!" interrupted the cow, "it is hard to think that a human would talk to us, you have never dealt with us in a matter in which you would differentiate us from beasts. You were kinder than others, certainly, but we thought you spoke to yourself through all these years."

"Look, Sir," the pig demanded, "the pastures are partly green now, and the sun shines, winter did not abate and threatens to come back with more downpour but let us enjoy this sunny day, you must be in our gratitude for we have awakened you in this lovely hour."

Mr. Mime took a deep breath, "it is a beautiful day indeed." He took a long careful look to a nonexistent thing in the horizon and smiled, "tell me, friends, do you know of a natural-born engineer? Someone or something who is born to build by default. We need to rebuild the doors for the barn."

"Beavers!" exclaimed the pig.

"Bravo, my pink friend. Let's make our way to them at once." The farmer hastily dressed in an unfashionable attire, before leaving, he left his wife a meal, kissed her cheek and went on his merry way with a good feeling in his chest, maybe his luck was changing, or perhaps it was the warm breakfast making its way to an empty stomach. A long journey awaited, the river was at least a quarter of a day's journey long and he had to walk there.

He had reached the riverbanks in what he estimated to be noon, for he and the animals that accompanied him worked according to daylight but not the human conception of time; sun meant work and play, moon meant sleep. To no one's surprise, the assiduous beavers were already there working on a dam. They were impeccable in executing a design they had not agreed on but came to them naturally. Twigs and branches were held behind their two massive well sharpened iron teeth. They worked without pause, if snow blocked their way, they would make way. Sedulous in their motion, their paddle-shaped tails danced behind them. Each had a task, or perhaps a preoccupation; some ate their leaves which they have preserved in the cold waters beneath, others' teeth were gnawing at a tree bark making sure the cuts he made were in opposition to the wind for the tree to fall, and other smaller ones were carrying the branches to the dam with their mouths, swimming with it was far easier than carrying it on land for they considered water their second home and their webbed feet made swimming as easy as walking. Stones and boulders were at the base of it all, then the heavy logs were placed, then the mud was placed on its walls.

"The timber must be interlocked," demanded one father to his children, "and mud must be dredged from the bottom of the river to properly seal the cracks."

"We know, father," said a child.

"I know you know, but I want to see that you know. No lollygagging!"

"I never understood the point of these dams, father," said another child.

"We need them so we could have more water to swim in to get to our food sources. Some of us work on the dam, others on digging tunnels. See, our work was done in autumn, but the last bear attack left us helpless. Usually, these large monsters hibernate during this time of year, and usually our dams could defy their attacks, but this year was different."

The father, upon seeing the human approach, warned his children of incoming danger and dipped into the waters out of the sight of the human. Mr. Mime sat down at the riverbank and waited to no avail; a few moments passed until he could see a brown figure laying in the snow beneath rays of sun that made their way through the intertwined branches above her. He approached her and spoke,

"Why don't you run away with the others?"

"Why would I? you would be doing me a favor in taking my life."

"But I am not a threat. I have come to ask you for a favor."

"I would help if you could bring my son back."

"Where is he now?"

"He was lost in the bear attack. Some witnesses claimed they saw his body go down the steam," she lamented, "why me, why must my son be a victim amongst all others."

"Would you rather some other child went missing? That would be cruel."

"Life is cruel, life is cruelty with an abundance of injustice."

"If life is unjust to all of us, dear friend, then life is just. Along the way I have learned that my bird friend who stands now on my shoulder lost her child as well. And so have I." The beaver looked at the bird and at the man in an equal measure of uncaringness, it seemed that the tragedy of others did not assuage one's own tragedy.

"Get me my son, alive or dead, and at once I shall begin building a door fitting for royalty."

From afar, two figures that looked like shadows seemed to observe closely the farmer. They have agreed that if it were true that the man speaks to animals, he would serve a purpose beyond his plebian occupation whatever it may be, if not, he is mad, and their time would not be wasted for they would enjoy following him just for the sake of entertainment. The man went to where the bear hibernated, the observers watched, calling him mad but without interrupting him. He walked into the cave, there were two cubs and their mother sleeping the winter away. The man interrogated the bear, demanding the truth about what happened.

"Have you eaten the child of the beaver? Answer me truthfully."

"Life is cruel, life is cruelty with an abundance of injustice. Does this answer your question?"

"Nay, it does not."

"Look around the cave, hunter," said the mother bear without truly waking up. Her eyes slept as her mouth moved, "I have two mouths to feed. Three, if I were to count myself. You do not understand what it means to take care of life, only taking it."

"I am a farmer, and I have lived from the bountiful earth without once shedding blood, even when I had the chance to do so, I have refused. You may close your eyes, but I know you are afraid that judgment has come, especially that it has come from someone so much feebler than you. The beaver demands your child as sacrifice, and I shall take him to her to do with it as she pleases."

Before the mother could roar or plead, the man had taken one of the two cubs to the bereaved beaver as a sacrificial lamb.

"Here it is, your chance to retaliate."

Before the beaver could open her mouth, before she could even make a judgment in her muddled thoughts dancing chaotically between anger and despair, a spirit came along. It was part opaque, part translucent, the colorless rays of sunlight turned green passing through it and reflecting on the river's surface like a glittering emerald whose voice emanated from the specters moving jaw.

"We were on the brink of starvation, and nothing was offered to us in terms of food and nutrition before the chill of winter. It took us off guard knowing well that we were not tardy, but the spring and summer of yesteryear were barren and famish would meet us at the horizon, twilight after twilight. We have travelled far and wide, taking great strides to nowhere, the circus would not give us food even if we agreed to be domesticated, and the priests would not give us an insignificant remnant of leftovers even if we agreed to be christened and baptized. Outside the human world, even this fallen Eden had little to offer." There was silence, the spirit had hoped the flesh mannequins of man and animal understood her plight. "If you spare my child, I promise to awaken myself at once and leave, burning what little energy we have, me and my little ones. We may die on the way in finding new shelter, but I would take the option of dying with my family one and all over you drowning my little one in this freezing pond." She held her silence for a moment before her soliloquy ended with one last line, "I have already lost a son this winter, I do not wish to lose another."

The wind blew through the specter, the man watched in disbelief with the cub in his hands as they grew wearier with each passing moment, the beaver stood unfazed even after witnessing the supranatural affair.

"This all means nothing, murderess," replied the beaver. Her lengthy diatribe was met with a single uncaring line, followed by a question, "lend us your wisdom, man. What shall I do?"

"You both suffer. Life is cruel and unjust, but we do not have to succumb to its cycle of violence. Hatred begets hatred, love

begets love, and mercy begets mercy. I have witnessed a war that
had begun over a murder from a single royal family, it grew, spi-
raling and snowballing through an incline that has no end, and a
hundred years have passed since. It started with my father, and it
did not end with my son. Perhaps the truth was lost and now the
story of the beginning of the war has changed but knowing that a
war that includes many nations and people could have been avoided
with forgiving the murder of one person breaks my heart. I would
say forgive, but I do not know much, I am not a learned man but
an observant one. Humans call me simple, and I would not like to
be anything else, and this is merely my opinion as a simple man."
He added, "she had already lost a child, it is true that her erratic
decision was asinine, but she had to think about her child, and her
options were limited. Very few vegetation lives in this time of year,
flesh was her only alternative."

"Listen," added the spirit, seeing that the beaver could understand the situation they were in but not willing to forgive just yet,
"I know of a spell, it could turn your sons' bones into a tree that
would grow the instant it is planted in the soil."

The beaver hesitated. "Present these seeds at once," she said
demandingly, the bear began to speak,

> "Exalted, inviolate,
> the skies turn violet,
> the earth shall breathe.
>
> Lifeless reverie,
> the sharpening of the tree,
> put the mind at ease.

From the metaphysical scatter,
from the mind, into matter,
I moldeth thee.

Taken asunder,
from an unseen blunder,
a mothers sacredness.

Rivers of tear meander,
my dear salamander,
into forgottenness.

She opened her eyes and proceeded with the
incantation,

"Tortured twigs and sprawling seas,
they all reside in me,
and I, myself, will die
leaving behind this tree.

Branches as bones, leaves as limbs,
this life doth not forsake.
As you have taken your dying breath,
the breath of death we take.

Mud and blood, yea and more
hearkens back the days of yore
with a heavy breath and deep sigh
you will arise, and I shall die.

Lo and behold, the green figure produced seeds made from her
sons' bones. The beaver eagerly grabbed the seeds with her two

front webbed paws and dug a small circle in the ground in which the seeds lay. A shallow coat of dirt would cover them before a giant tree emerged. It went as far as the eye could see, stretching into the heavens momentarily with a trunk with a diameter of an ancient cedar and branches that reached out to hug the surrounding oaks. The tree was evergreen and could feed the beavers for all eternity. The mother cried bitter tears and knelt, kissing the exposed roots that hung above ground. She knew her kind would feed from it when the next season came, and she did not mind. There was silence. A deal was sealed in which all parties emerged, perhaps not satisfied with the hand of fate, but they had to make do for they had agreed to an unwritten contract, and each kept their end. From a distance, a mother bear with one child fled their den as the other was rudely awakened, scurried away to join them. They walked away into what seemed to be certain death with a silent glance of goodbyes, not for the merciful beings but perhaps for the world itself. The beaver called for her tribe to work on the door and greet the stranger in need. The watchers from afar looked in disbelief at the events that unfolded, they looked at each other to reaffirm one another that they witnessed truly the event as they conspired. They followed the man as noon was turning into dawn and the sun sunk itself into a bathe of cool ocean water. The door was erected by the barn animals before they marched in bidding the farmer farewell. Mr. Mime went home, leaving behind the awestruck priests who were ready to tax the poor fellow but in seeing what he has accomplished changed their minds, a man like him could serve them well, but the watchers approached him before the robed men.

"Sir, we have been watching you from afar," said one.

"Simply unbelievable, yet undeniable," said another.

"This will cause alarums and excursions like no other," said one.

"A ballyhoo, a blather, a bluster. Call it what you will," said another.

"How may I help you gentlemen?" asked cordially the protagonist.

"Let us introduce ourselves proper. This man here, my fellow skeptic, his name is."

"Callum of Claistero," interrupted the man, "son of the late count."

"I have heard about your father. He was a great man," stopped the farmer to bow.

"Oh no, dear friend, people like you, we shake their hands," and so they did.

"I am Robert Ebert. Author, partly famous."

"Emphasis on partly," said Callum.

"Funny. Very funny, I would end this persiflage by saying no. Nay, it is not funny. See," explained Robert, "I took our haughty, naughty, and bumptious friend here for a walk to show him the grand works of God manifesting in nature a notion he rejects with every part of his being."

"I still do. But I must say you, Sir, serve as a reminder. A reminder that we are at the top of the food chain, we have nature's neck on a leash, and we must teach it a few tricks, to serve us of course. We have pursued the scientific method to its extreme and yet nature keeps offering obstacles. This, what you have done today, I dare say this is beyond our understanding. We have cut many animals to learn their anatomy to learn about them, yet you speak to them like man would to his fellow."

"Odd," said the man, "have you tried not cutting them?"

"Hah," guffawed the limited crowd, "this man is a weisenheimer."

"Funny," answered his mate, "and smarter than we think, it seems."

"I think, maybe it's the mutual respect I have with nature. I would not know; I say this in earnest."

"Respect?" answered the alarmed Callum, "diseases and death, animal excrement and the bony remains of our ancestors, filth and ailments, ants and hornets, things that crawl and things that fly, things that gnaw at you from earth or sky and they all hate you equally, they all want to kill you. That is nature, and it is not worthy of our respect."

"I could swear that this is not my experience with it. Well, perhaps only partly," answered Mime.

"May we ask why you have embarked on this adventure and why?" asked Callum.

"My wife is sterile. We have lost our only son in the war. The rest of details you would not believe even if I told you."

"Just so it happens, we do have the best physicians. It's no exaggeration really, perhaps on earth I dare say. Come with us, tell us your tales, and in return we shall help your wife in any way we can. You are well connected to nature, we are well connected to science, we shall help each other."

The man arrived to his doorless house. His wife was shivering beneath her covers in the chill of the night. His companions patiently waiting outside. Mr. Mime sat on his side of the bed and decided to bring solace to his inconsolable wife, "even if another child was born from your womb, how would it replace your own?" he awaited a reply before continuing, "you can have another child, you can track and kill the man who had taken his life, but nothing will bring him back. If he will not return the same man as he left, then he will not return at all." He grabbed her hand, their fingers intertwined in the empty spaces between each individual bone, "nothing will bring him back. We should not look for replacements.

There are no replacements." He sat in silence, thinking about what else there was to say, but there was nothing else.

"For an idiot," she pouted, pulling herself out of bed like an ancient statue that decided one day to set its stones in motion, her breath smelled of death for she was still fasting, "you are wise, and beyond brave."

"Come with me love," he spoke, half demandingly, half pleadingly, "come with me."

"There's nowhere else I would rather be than next to you." In the stillness of the night, they made their way to the prestigious university of Vardinberg, along the way the learned men discussed whether it was a good idea dragging two people of such social stature with them.

"At best," argued Robert to his skeptic friend, "we acquire a knowledge of arcane and esoteric origins. It gives us bragging rights in this life, and eternal remembrance once we're gone, if not, it could serve as a collection of tales whose imagination knows no bounds. We have nothing to lose."

Chapter Eight

NATURE TAKES
ITS COURSE

It had gotten colder by the second. The more they traveled west, the more the wind pushed back in an eastwardly direction, pleading them not to pursue this lost cause. The father, the husband, or the pigeon in question was far away in a place unknown, a place not of their own nor was it one they knew. The falcon had guided them true but there was a danger looming in. Nature had its laws, and these laws had few exceptions, few anomalies that seldom happened, and a foremost law all living things knew was as such: prey and predator shall not walk along each other, nor fly, swim, or crawl. In case they met, only one or the other shall remain. Yet, here was the golden bird guiding them through the winter's cloud and they, in their desperation, followed. It was a cause of great concern, a great alarm, and the family in its entirety wished to retreat to where they came from, but it was too late now, far too late. Their flapping wings did not abate, yet they greatly tired in an adventure that felt endless. Sue's maternal instincts caused her great distress, "what shall happen to my little ones, this is a fool's errand." Many other whispers in her ears she did not vocalize, for their guide was ever silent and she was not willing to interrupt. The energy preserved was needed to fly, to escape, if need be, at any moment her tale could end tragically.

They flew for days. The pigeons ate what little food nature and man had to offer along the way from forgotten grains and breads by the soldiers to some odd winters' fruits here and there. They were not picky eaters, and every time they fed, she noticed the falcon did not eat for most of their food was indigestible to him, nor did he go hunting which was a cause of great concern. There was very little wildlife; white furred rabbits and dears he had missed, perhaps, she told herself, he fed while they slept. She had hoped so at least. His insatiable hunger was obvious, his eyes once focused on the sky in motion, now he was looking at birds that accompanied him, his looks were bereft of innocence, they were the looks she had afeared to witness ever since their travel had begun. She was alert and in turn alerted her children to stay a few inches back. It all happened so suddenly, yet foreseen and expected. The grand golden-brown wings of the predator froze up like a wall hanging midair. He was now behind them, looking carnivorously at the subject of his hunt. There was no safety in the sky, she thought. Quickly, she instructed her young ones to dive headfirst into the malleable earth for there was nowhere to hide in midair, no cloud would conceal them for too long. Their swift descent had commenced, like a crash landing downwards into a white wasteland. There were no trees except two decayed trunks extending upwards, blackened, hollow, and unmendable they stood unalive, yet the roots clung firmly to the

damp soil. They headed towards them. They were barely ahead of
the monster that followed. She urged James to hang on tightly for
he still rode on her back. All three pilots splashed into the snow,
but the falcon was dizzy from the blistering freefall whilst on an
empty stomach. He crashed into one of the two dead woods and
a splatter of blood and splinters followed. The blood was his own.
He did not awaken.

Enfeebled were the children by the shocking ordeal, Robin
cried bitter tears over their guide as he tried to reawaken him with
the softest of touches, as if alert of his murderous intent and yet
he would not let him die. Sue begged him to leave the body alone.

"Why do you cry over the body of your enemy?" she asked dryly.

"He saved me," he flatly replied without breath.

"He also tried to kill you," she rebuked her eldest son, "or have
you forgotten from what we have escaped what seemed to be certain
death?"

"How will we get to father now?" he breathed out his question
as interludes between suffocating cries. This journey was difficult
for the little ones, they were new to flight and to the brutal ways
of the unmerciful nature, Rosy joined into the cacophony of wails,
"how will we get to father now?" This she did not answer, nor
could she, she was as lost as her children. "How will we get to father now?" cried the children, exhaustion had depressed the young
travelers, but their mother kept a brave face about, for everyone's
sake. Her youngest who sat on her back shook the snow off his little
yellow coat, he did not join the crying crowd but asked in genuine
curiosity, "what now, mother?"

"Oh dear. Oh, my dearest, now we wait for them to catch their
breath, we can't reason with them while they're suffocating. You,
my youngest, are the bravest of them all and yet you cannot spread
your wings yet. We shall wait for them to gather their strength and

we shall be on our way at once. Eventually, your siblings will realize that such happenstance will frequently occur on their lonesome, this journey could serve as an educational trial, I think. I...I hope it does." The featherless one nodded.

From the other trunk intact emerged a figure whose body was concealed, whose only obvious traits were its eyes; they were those of a cat. He yawned and stretched his paws. His inquisitive stare at once caught the presence of the pigeon family. The cautious mother exclaimed at the sight of him "Stay back!" cried Sue, "I have dealt with one too many a predator today." She would fly if she could, but her children were in a sorry state of sobs, and she herself was fatigued beyond the ability of flight, all she could do was somehow awkwardly shoo the cat away.

"Relax," said Snowfluff, "I am a well-fed housecat, the last thing my stomach desires would be some leathery fleshed vermin," he concluded as he yawned. He observed daylight absorbingly, looking towards the heavens and squinting his freshly awakened yet still drowsy eyes. He looked around then paused calculatingly, he had seen the golden feathers before, "I have seen your kind before. Yes, two of them to be precise, a male and a female. You're one of those glorified messengers 'innit?"

Her heart sunk; it plunged to her feet and her lungs could not draw in breath, "M-male, you say? Where? Where did you see him? Show me at once?"

"This way," he turned and walked towards the encampment. With the first few steps he had taken, the wife followed automatically looking for her husband, in the despairing desire to find him, deductive thinking was no longer an option. She was victim to the ebb and flow of life's tidal waves and all the helplessness that it entails, even her children broke from their wails to warn her. "Mother," they said together, "are you really going to go through this again?" She turned briefly and looked at them without disappointment, without admonishment, without any form of judgement. Wordlessly, she turned back without commanding them to follow, but they followed anyways. Fear accompanied them along the way, it had possessed them, turning them more akin to puppets rather than free willed animals. It was hard to hope for a dream within this nightmare, but perhaps, thought their mother, perhaps the worst had already passed. The massive Maine Coon was at least five times their collective size, there was an impossibility in fending off any aggression he could potentially incite. She prayed for the goddess and walked with her kids. In fear, their wings reached out haphazardly and impulsively to touch hers. She grabbed them firmly and they formed a chain. Their little legs left miniscule prints in the snow.

The encampment was torn to shreds by the claws of some monstrosity. The beds were mauled and shewed upon. The pillows torn with feathers hanging out like blood and organs would from a biological organism, no food remained nor has there been any sign of life. They were all in shock. The cat had lost its owner, or slave as he saw him to be, and the pigeons' quest to find their husband and father was equally futile. No time for tears or lamentations was there, a new blizzard was peeping through the veil of space and decided to descend. They camped inside the ruins.

"I know how it looks like," said the cat, "out of the frying pan and into the fire, but I would not hurt you. I too have lost someone dear to me. We lived here together for as long as I can remember, and now he is gone, and so is everyone else but he is all that matters to me. I will find him," by seeing how calm she was, he was certain she was not as collected nor as tranquil as she seemed to be, "you will find whoever you are looking for too. We are on the right track, and you have, through blind luck or through the will of some deity, found just the right animal. I know where my friend lives and I have memorized the route to him. We shall find him, and in turn you shall find what you are looking for. I'll help if you help, and as the old saying goes, scratch my back and I'll scratch yours."

She nodded. Her alert eyes moved stiffly within their skull as they cautiously tracked the predators every move as the outer white blanket grew thicker with snowflakes so grand it looked as if the clouds tore themselves to shreds and fell.

Chapter Nine

FREEDOM

For days, he would toil. His hands were covered with mud, soil, and blood from the ceaseless drudgery bestowed upon him by Father Jeremiah. Yes, the motion he engaged in resembled his past work so much that it engaged memories he had willingly forgotten, or so he thought, not because they were unpleasant, which they were to their very core, but because he felt pity for the old fool; unvocal pity, but unequivocal love and respect. He never knew comfort. Leisure was a concept so strange and so alien to him. He looked at the crowd as if they were mad every instance in which they were drunk, or merrymaking, or drunk in merrymaking. For his entire life, his head stooped as low as his chest, if not in his study reading of some book or another, it was in the land bending his back forward as low as he could in harvest or in sowing. He did not subjugate the young Sebastian in any way, but the guilt the young man felt looking at him imposed upon him a sense of obligation. He did not know, nor does he now know why. He trained him in field work, in the ways of combat, in the ways of learned men, reading and writing, the cordialities and formalities of royalty and the vulgarities of the commoners. Indeed, he learned what he needed to know and more. He slept two hours a day and ate only his fill. His provisions were provided by his supervisor, his overseer who also was his father figure, his mentor, his friend, and his plight, as if he were pandoras box opened for the sake of some forgotten diamond within. The young orphan looked at his father in reverence so great that he could deify him, Jeremiah could see it and at once he commanded him, "put your trust in God alone, for men are bound to two things, failure and death." Those words were not uplifting to him. He wanted a hero he could see, a hero he could touch and hug in times of despair and hardship. His reality traversed a certain unconscious dreamscape in which it jolted, metamorphosizing between the now and then, the where and when, his fatigue would not allow him to work, and his master did not allow him to sleep, torturing herself in return. Her wrath and brooding mood were contagious and he himself suffered psychologically with her, for emotions are transferred in humans from one to another. He waited for her to calm down, but the storm in her heart never faltered; within her there was thunder, rain, and an all-consuming hurricane.

Days would pass, and nights would end, no solace would God send their way, their fates were now as intertwined as mating serpents. He waited, for as long as he would wait before the storm would abate. More suns and more moons until some early days of June, it was then that her hardened heart of stone within its chest of ailing burdened bones took pity. She unwrapped his chains and unshackled his feet, his fetters were no more. He had forgotten the sweetness of freedom and sat silently on his wooden board which he considered a bed. He waited. Perhaps, there was a mistake, perhaps she would change her mind, until her mouth spoke those words, "kill me," she demanded, "free me as I have freed you for no solace has yet come my way." "Milady," he answered after what seemed to be speechless years, "I would die before witnessing a thorn prickle your finger." He held her with his emaciated arms whose strength and vigor had been drained, yet they firmly grabbed unto the inflictor of their downfall. She cried bitterly over his chest, the tears trickling down like a flood gate had been released from her sorrowful half-shut eyes. It took from daylight till nightfall until her nerves were calmed and her forgiveness accepted. What were they to do now? With forgiveness granted mutually, all that remained was forgetting, to truly move on, and move away from their defaced fates. To distance themselves from hurtful memories made, they realized they would distance themselves from the places in which these memories were made. A week was spent in each other's arms, telling tall tales of heroic adventures and promises of making things right with not-so-subtle hints of romance thrown in for good measure. It happened suddenly and naturally, like an erupting volcano or geyser, they have loved one another.

"Would you return and tell your father to wed us?" she asked.

"My father? Oh no, I realize it is far better for me to send him a letter, as depressing as it may seem. If I go back now, there would be no return."

"I would not go back either...you know why."

"I know."

"I had to witness my comrades abandon me. The life of my son was worth as little as a hundred silver coins. I would never. I would kill them if I ever saw them again. I would kill them all."

"I know." He kissed her forehead and waited for her to speak as she took a moment of silence in remembrance of that day.

"Maybe he could come to us?" she asked.

"He is imprisoned, no bribe would free him. A prisoner is one thing, a royal prisoner is another, and it is not as regal nor as luxurious as it sounds."

"We need to leave, the earlier the better."

"Yes, let me write him merely to inform him and inform the king as well of my departure."

"The king? are you mad? I swear you do sound like a gullible knave at time. What for?"

"I am sworn to honor my duty for the king."

"He does not need to know. Please, he might conspire against you."

"This is about honor."

She distanced herself from him, pacing around the room with anxious steps, with the absence of back and forth in dialogue. She took large strides that that took her nowhere as if standing in her place. She tried not to scream, it did not take long for her to fail such a task, "honor!" she exclaimed, "what fairy tale! What nonsense! What hideous nonsense, you child-like men with big armors of steel and heads bloated with tall tales of chivalry tell yourselves. Chivalry would be the end of you. You would die for a thing most forgotten, if ever it did exist."

"Honor is all there is," his dry voice croaked laconically, "I live by it and die for it." In her doubtful eyes, he saw his words were not affecting her, "it is the same honor that made me live under your roof and your command for months without me going mad and, God forbid, hurting you, or even just fleeing away, far away from here. I was in chains, but the weight of those chains of metal are worth their weight in gold. All pain and agony are mental attributions I have forsook for the sake of honor. If the world is without honor, then it is not that honor that does not exist, it is that the world lives in dishonor."

Acrimony and maliciousness made way to her heart, a feeling manifested in her eyes with force, she stepped forwards towards him. One step, two steps, the third she could not take. Some other sense was obstructed, nay, it was stricken with a force like that of a charging bull.

"What is that smell?" she asked, "is that...is that you?"

"Well, you would not let me bathe, so now you reap the consequences. Personally, I have grown accustomed to the smell."

"Oh lord, lord have mercy." she closed her nose, but that did not help her a bit, "begone from my sight, there is a bathtub in the barn."

"The barn!" he protested.

"Shush, yes, the barn. Go now, I'll follow soon with hot water and hyssop deodorant, and I think, I think I have some spare Castille soap somewhere." Her eyes drifted about in search for some item until they fixated upon him for one last command as her breath shortened, "go. Now!"

He left with a smile on his face. He was glad to finally bathe from all the filth he had wallowed in. Just like breaking a long fast, the feeling of sweet release was finally upon him, and it felt better than ever. Margaret bathed him. Those who walked by would send disagreeing glances until one of them spoke

"You lust after your kin slayer, wench!" she laughed it off, and with the clamoring crowd as witness she called him out, "and you lust after your goats." That was the end of their exchange. Sebastian guffawed and caressed her hair; he closed his eyes and recited his words as if memorized and she would write them down and attach them, through the letters, on her pigeon's chest. At once, it flew until invisible.

"Is it sent?" he asked, and she nodded He closed his eyes and opened his mouth, "we are officially living on borrowed time. Let us depart at once."

"Why?" her hagride vocals rung in question, "what happens now?"

"My request for freedom is declined, and my body is pierced, torn with the sharpest of weapons, except if we make our way to shore in one piece and as soon as possible. It took us four days on horse to arrive here, yes?"

"True."

"Then, it takes the bird a single day to get to our point of departure. How long will it take us to make our way for the shore?"

"Half a day, or so I estimate."

"Good," he stated, not with excitement nor melancholy but rather in a very matter-of-factly manner. "Good. Whatever satchels, bags, pockets, and all that could conceal essential items, fill them now and we shall carry them with us," she hastened. The knight dried his body and with the lack of alternatives he quickly wore his befouled garments. They rode through a lot, both had suffered numerous indignations, humiliations, and with the unceasing gallops of their trusty steed the end was in sight. They were welcomed at the finish line with the iodine breath of the sea and the patina of its otherworldly quaintness, and the abundance of life and death concealed within it. It congregated all. Yes, the air was different here, and so were the people; they were prosperous. The roads were clean, the bodies were hygienic, but they could not scrub away the smell of the ocean and its bountiful mermaid womb. Fish of all shapes and colors were on display, the alien flesh of the saltwater inhabitants demanded their appetizing attention.

In the dark pit that served as a place of respite and simultaneously a prison for the priest, his light was obstructed by a passing bird returning to a small opening in the ground from which little blades of evening light cut through. He obstructed them and, at once, the priest noticed him standing and peeking politely, it was an honest gesture, a gentle reminder of him having company. "Come hither, love," said he, and it went towards him, "you poor thing. Your wings are about to get crystallized from the frost. Here," he grabbed it in his hands and brought him closer to the light of the candle he had been granted by the executioner as reward for his meek demeanor, "here, this should be better." The all-surrounding still blackness was cold and motionless, but he resided in this small dancing halo whose warmth was insignificant but adequate between two firm hands whose skin was tough but intentions pure. The priest took off the letter from the pigeon's chest and put him closer to the flickering candlestick. He spoke to him like an old friend and confidant, "they lie; they lie and demand honesty, and once I was honest, I wounded up here, with new wounds on an older body. Tell me, how could they demand a virtue as sacred as honesty and act with such deceit and mendacity? If the truthful should be punished, the liar shall prevail, why would one suffer for virtue?" said Jeremiah, "I thought I was helping, but perhaps these people do not need help. They do not bite the hands that feeds, but shower the hands that strangle them with kisses, and I am starting to wonder if they deserve...nay, I shall not fill my head with such thoughts." He bowed his head in a crestfallen manner. Noticing another letter on the pigeon's chest with a red wax seal, he said, "do not carry my burdens with you for then you cannot fly. Go. Hurry, you need to leave."

A voice ululated from the echoing darkness. The emotions that danced with it were hard to dissect, but they seemed to mock, yes, mockery was the most prevalent chord that was struck with the singing voice, "have you lost your mind man? You speak to a bird!"

"Not any bird; a pigeon."

"What difference does it make?"

"They carry letters with them all the time. They are Godsent messengers blessed by Noah himself. If they carry words written, why then would they not carry words said?"

The voice roared in amusement; with sufficient warmth gathered in his small body, the pigeon was ready to be dispatched again through the hole in the ceiling. The priest received letter of his son leaving, he wept bitterly in his cell. He knew he was as good as dead and prayed for his safe passage. Before letting the bird to leave the side of the small dying fire, he begged him, "if he is to make it out alive, return to me, if not then leave eternally." It was then that the bird was set free.

His fluttering wings made way to inside the castle. In the hall of the King, Edward had already signed the death warrant of Sir Sebastian. The man who would bring his head would be rewarded with as many bounties that would please his greedy soul. The pigeon was in the pen when the declaration was signed and sealed. Melvin saw the crimson wax and asked.

"Who from was the letter?"

"A knight by the name of Sebastian. I have heard him say he was going to start anew with his life in some uncharted place far away, he might leave the kingdom to somewhere else, maybe even get married to woman who saved him, or whom he saved, I did not really know."

"You fool," ejaculated Melvin, "you fool! The man is as good as dead. He is going nowhere."

"No one blames you," interrupted Susan, "it happens often."

"Are they really going to kill him? He is the bravest man to walk the earth, or so I have heard."

"Yes, and he wants to leave the service of the king. This means the end of him."

"There is no stopping it now. And you cannot stay here, nor are you allowed to run away from your duties. That would be blasphemous."

The caretaker grabbed the visitor and sent it away with an order to assassinate the renegade soldier. In less than a day the dispatched order was in their hands, they dispersed in search for the knight nd his wife-to-be. The people in question were lost with the sights and sounds and smells of the place; the sense of adventure was throttling in full force towards them with the many dangers and hopes and dreams that loomed about. The assassins might be making their way from the castle walls, the ship they were to board may crash, the land they were to reach may be hostile. But it did not matter, they were together now, whatever came their way, and come what may, they were ready. They conversed in the room of the cheapest inn they could find.

"You have spoken to the captain, yes?"

She nodded, "sure thing. We depart first thing tomorrow. He knows of our urgent situation and promises to embark as soon as he could. You could have sent your letter from here, you know."

"How? by whose birds? Your pigeon was far more trustworthy; he also knows the lay of the land. The feral ones scattered here would not know their way to the place I call home."

"You don't know that."

"It does not matter love, what is done is done."

She sighed and grabbed him in fear, "perhaps. Death follows a knight where he goes, our situation now is no different. How do you get used to it?"

"Death is to kill for, and peace is to die for."

"Yes, sure, keep telling yourself these nonsensical aphorisms. I swear, you and your stories would be the end of me."

"Stories are everything my love. We do not exist in our bodies but the tales that we leave behind. I have seen many men die, but the great ones live on posthumously. The mediocre and the weak achieve nothing and pass from this mortal coil as if nothing happened, and they are shocked that no one wants to hear their stories, and in turn reject stories in which what they consider impossible, an impossible that had been achieved. We are worth little more than the tales we tell, and most are shocked that they have lost their worth for their stories are not worth hearing. Mark my words, whatever happens, ballads will sing our song, it will have your name and mine. I just hope to live to hear it, and I know you want to hear them too."

She sounded some grievances he did not hear and slept in his arms. He stayed dressed and awake all night to see the early dusk come and save them, he never felt fear for his life before, but in his hands, he had a treasure that made the bravest man shake in his boots in fear of losing it, someone to care for in a knight's worldview is someone to die for. Daylight descended like a savior from the heavens. It took him a while to awaken himself, stupor sat on his eyelids like a demon, but his eyes were still wide-open. He gently shook her awake at earliest he could and in moribund motion detached his back from the comfortless mattress. They rushed to the docks and met the captain on shore, but a danger was looming and from nowhere in particular did they emerge until they heard the hostile voices.

"They're already here!" exclaimed she, dreading her fate and clutching unto her many bags.

"We always were here, woman. We never left. It comes always to our advantage when you folks forget."

"The eyes of Edward are ever-present everywhere," said another thug, "as for you, Sebastian, remember your oath and come back home, or die where you stand."

The gallant knight sheathed his sword and said, "give us no quarter, for we shall grant you none." Immediately, swords clashed in a deadly dance, bystanders watched in horror, some in fear, others relished in their entertainment. The first fiend dropped dead. Sebastian equipped himself with a halberd, the knight hastily took it from the defiled dead hands of his enemy, his weapon of choice trumped any other he possessed. It's true that she had forgiven him, but in seeing him with a halberd in his hands, her fury was scorched, and she fought like a thousand suns with her dagger, she could not escape the haunting memory that dawned on her as he held the weapon from the fallen assassin, the name of her son shone in her head like a signal of pain. This made her question to what extent had she truly forgiven, but this was no time for questions and contemplations. The fight raged on, and no authorities would interfere, this was a prosperous town and there was mostly no need for violence, they certainly were not prepared for carnage so grand in scale. The enemies of the fleeing duo dropped like flies until none remained on their feet. She made her way onboard, forgetful of her possessions. She expected him to follow her with them so she could castigate him for his past, but he would not make it before an arrow from a distant bowman made its way to his chest, and another cracked open his skull with its sharp steel tip releasing from his flesh like goo through his eye socket from which a fountain of blood emerged. His death was imminent, and perhaps painless, the pain that was left to be felt was that of the survivor. The body dropped unto its knees, as if fighting to stay upright and witness the ship depart from the horizon and away from sight to bid it Godspeed, a sight it did not possess. Bystanders dispersed hurryingly, and the coward descended to collect the bounty of his successful hunt. The motionless limbs of the statuesque man were disregarded by the many bodies of citizens who rushed by it, some affirmed its existence from first glance and at once fled, others had to look twice to reaffirm their disbelief, such violence never occurred in their lands. As the victor descended, he shot another arrow towards her direction but managed to shoot the ship's hull alone. He tried to shoot again yet missed, her swift motion had saved her, yet she could not outrun the sorrow setting in like a demonic possession. She collapsed aboard the deck; beneath the tearful eyes her vision was misty black. Waterdrop following waterdrop, into the rippling raging sea. There came a thunder from afar, a mad god rubbed the clouds the way a primal ape rubbed his flints eons ago in the iota of history and the stars stood in line in respect, like candles in a silent vigil.

Days would pass as time stood still for her, the shining sun and the glowing moon did not console her, nor did they try. In his rotting pit, the priest stood and sat and slept looking through the hole in the ceiling until his neck had grown stiff and immovable. The bird never returned. It rained down unto his neck and well beneath until his eyes were dry.

Chapter Ten

FOUND

They were lost in the aftermath of the blizzard. There were no tracks to follow, everything was concealed, cloaked beneath the snow. Running away would be far easier this time around but she had to be always cautious, and so she let the cat lead the way. There was nothing in sight that could give any indication of their whereabouts, no landmarks, nothing that stood out except in the unlikely event in which they could see themselves. They walked round and round. They walked until Snowfluff realized that he saw paws printed in the surface. They were his own.

"Hopeless," he lamented, "it is all hopeless, we're no better than a dog chasing his tail." One despairing glance he sent towards the family before he disappeared, submerging in the snow. Sue and her children flew above the ground, hovering in search for him, she would not take chances in trusting a predator so agile that could lunge so high he could even now reach them. She looked below, but there he was, he did not move but laid flat on his belly and had his paws covered his crying eyes.

"I should never have left him," he said, sensing the pigeon closing in, "I had everything I could wish for, and now, for one single incident, a short outburst of anger, I am here. I took things far too personally; he was a busy man, my mast...my slave. There is no escaping this white maze, this white tomb, there is no escape!"

"Come now, get a hold of yourself you over-fluffed fool. We need to leave, and time is not on our side."

"Why don't you fly away?"

"In which direction? I have never been to Callistero."

"Nor would I know how to guide you, I am as lost as a drifting leaf in the wind."

She looked around before an idea came to her, "the tent was of military use. There should be a map, naturally."

"Yes, I believe I saw shreds of it here and there. It is torn to pieces as it is."

"Come with me." They retraced their steps to the point of departure and looked at the torn map which was on the wall with its parts scattered everywhere. Like a puzzle, they rearranged the pieces to the best they could. There were gaps, but their reconstruction was closer to perfection than they could have ever hoped for. Sue could read, and the cat sat on the snow it dragged in disbelief.

"Ok, we are," she hovered her right and pointed at the map, "here. And your friend resides right about... there." She pointed and the cat nodded in understanding. He did not feign interest, but his comprehension was counterfeit. "To my understanding, that is east... so." She turned around and pointed her beak, "we were traveling in the wrong direction. Now we know where to go, let us depart this instance."

"Wait. What about me?"

"You will come with us, obviously."

"Yes, but what if I lose sight of you in the sky? You cannot possibly give me a conclusive description of your aerial vision if all there is to be seen is uniform whiteness. Look, here's a chain I found, well a collection of chains really, my guess is they were supposed to take prisoners with them, but perhaps there were no prisoners to take. This is great! It really is, it means a lot of people are free now. I was thinking maybe you and your kids can carry it and I will follow the trail it should make in the snow."

"We can try." The three pigeons could carry the intertwined chains. It was a herculean endeavor but an achievable one. Eastwards pointed their eyes, and eastwards they flew with the cat jumping around the snow below at a snail like pace. They lost track of the cat along the way, but they were reassured as the chains extended to the ground and a trail made him a passage to their destination. Sue was in an awkward position; her children seemed to be more comfortable flying with the weight while she and her little resident on her back were struggling. She trudged as she carried both weights, and he was trying to balance himself upon his mother's back, for she flew in an upward motion, and he could not stand still with the billowing turbulence. James slipped and fell. The yellow piece of cloth glided in his descent like a miniature cape. He screamed along the way, but no sound made impact. The white particles broke his fall. He was discombobulated from fear as he witnessed the ground growing nearer and nearer. Pleasantly surprised by the lack of pain, he looked around to see a barren terrain and a family of pigeons that looked very much like his own, a mother and her two children, confused as to how they reached his whereabouts nut. In such a speed, he approached and without a word departed with them. Sue panicked and dropped the chain. In her mind, she trusted her children the way she trusted herself. They remained at a stable altitude but were going to join her before she protested. "No, I have a gut feeling, call it an instinct, that we are unbelievably close to your father. You follow the cat, and I will follow your brother. I have faith in you. Both of you. We shall meet where the chain marks end." She left them to take care of them, one trial that they have not yet passed was upon them now, it was the burden of responsibility. They went on their separate ways until their roads had reached their different conclusions. The siblings sat at the very threshold of the gates of the city awaiting the cat, and the mother reached the nest of the supposed kidnappers. The cat arrived and was greeted by the guard with warmth and pleasantries, he was hugged and pampered as he was carried to his rightful owner, and he was elated in his elevation for his tired legs no longer needed to touch the cold ground. The birds followed the guard with every step he took, until at last, at the very last they have seen their father in semi-nakedness. There, hanging in a pen in the corner of the bedroom in the master chamber in which the Countess and her husband to be slept. They hastened and pecked at the bars which held their father captive and seeing this at once Countess Claire called for her servant Alice to open.

"But he is not yet fully recovered" protested Krill.

"Look at them," she replied, "they must be related by blood, and they must be reunited."

"Oh well, I suppose so. Farewell, and prithee take care my precious quill." The lock cracked open by the turning key. "You shall be missed," he said as he set him free. The three birds flew out the window never to be seen again.

Sue, in her branching path, had another story to tell. She met the kidnappers as they made their way to their nest, and their nest was a mere part of a grand compound of nest built next to one another. She made sure not to test their ire, yet her maternal instincts drove her to confront them. They justified their wrongdoing with altruism and ulterior motives.

"We saw a child fall from the sky. We thought nothing of it and stepped in to save him. You are more than welcome." Sue approached steadily, but the soliloquy resumed as the speaker saw a threatening look embedded between the whites and blacks of her eyes, "you mutilate your children, but mutilate them with gold. You put them in the face of danger so treacherous one could consider it certain death but think of us as backwardly. Sure, go ahead and call us what you will, feral, animalistic, wild... but one must wonder, one must introspect about their own being at times. How many wars could you have prevented? How many betrayals? How many words of ill will and gossipmongering could you have put to an end? Your humans are malicious overlords, but you, do you think yourself bereft of responsibility if you send a letter that sparks anger, despair, or one that transcends the personal sphere and could drag an entire nation to war? You are just as responsible, and just as despicable as they. The messenger is nothing without their message, and a message would go nowhere without a messenger, rendering it ineffective. If the words were unheard and unread, even if written, they do not exist."

Without a word, she did not humor the stranger with her riddling questions, nor did she engage in debate, all she did was demand raucously, "hand over my child."

"Nay, he will choose." She blocked his path with her wing, his yellow cape covered his eyes in fear, "tell me, James, what would you like to do?"

He did not speak a word. Shyly, he tiptoed, making his way around her. He hugged his mother afraid, and without a word, they left.

They met at the crossroad were their paths forked but now

conjugated. The family was finally reunited with all its members. Sue, as eager as she was to kiss her beloved mate, said,

"explain yourself. And it better be a good explanation."

"We are royal messengers. The good news and the bad news both need to be delivered. The constable needed to write, so did the earl marshal, the crossbowmen, the provost marshal, the lieutenants, the knights, and the dregs of the foot soldiers in the infantry. In giving them my feathers, I was left naked in the shivering cold, I thought I saw Eleonore frequent the tent of the constable, but I can't be too sure, I was living in the most elegiac times of my life, I was in too much pain to see properly. They were kind enough to wrap and insulate me from the abhorrent weather. It was not until now that I have recovered, and my recovery is still not full, as you can see."

"Vainglory drives the males of the species. What did you think would happen to you, you fool? Did you think that some poet would write a song of your bravery and altruism and a bard would play it? The bird lost all his feathers that he could not fly home to his family. Brave beyond foolishness, and foolish beyond bravery. You…" She was out of words, and all she could do was look at him in pity, his sacrifice to others meant nothing to her, but his presence meant the world itself.

"Mother, where is your golden feather?" asked Rosy.

"I do not need it child, I have many others. and I was thinking, Nelson, maybe we should go feral."

"By the goddess, why?" he exclaimed.

"Come with me, and I'll show you. All of you, come along now. I shall explain along the way."

Chapter Eleven

POSTMORTEM PANDEMONIUM

The horse riders made their way through a part of the woods long forgotten; it was forbidden to enter there by some strange decision that no one has ever questioned before, for no one had their attention drawn to such a grotesque part of the woods, especially when they had an abundance of fertile soil where they lived. The trees there conspired against man. The infernal horror spewed beneath the earth with its green flame rising and sputtering. The roots extended into the lava and screamed in pain as they suckled on the bountiful sludge shaped minerals whilst eternally burning and eternally mending itself in its cyclical self-flagellation and imminent healing. Its twisted, tormented branches extended to one another and hand-in-hand joined in a deathly dance for the horrific williwaw of wind had a different tune here, it was that of terror. But of course, no one would know, no one would tread there, and even if they saw what they saw and were to report their findings they would be certainly dismissed as madmen. It was the land of the crows; they cawed at every corner, and he could sense their presence even though he saw not one.

Betwixt things were the dark grey ashen palettes, and there was a lonesome, singular pale figure miniscule and shrinking; it was that of Tobias. Upon seeing the frightening and sublime tree ahead, he knew it was their destination and froze in his place. "We have arrived," announced his companion. There was a restless silence within him, a demanding head would repeatedly tell him to retreat but his feet were planted as firmly as roots. It was a terrible thing, a titan in scale with an ivy of thorns like that of a euphorbia milli but thicker. It revolved around the trunk and pirouetted within itself and encompassed all things in its domain like a lover suspended pendulously from the branches, vacillating between its adoration and hatred for its partner. Its trunk was a thing to behold and a thing beholden, it could fit two sequoia trees in its diameter and its height he could not make out for there was no end to it in sight; it extended to the land of giants where Jack the thief made his fortune, and perhaps beyond that even. A congregation of men gathered, but he refused to be one of them. It was not until he was called for that he complied. To the behest of the demand from a source unknown, he stepped forward. It had spoken, "the man in tawdry metal so thin it would not save him from a fleeting wind, come now, see me as I see you." The voice was certainly not human, but as if some natural element parroted these words, uncanny as it he heeded the command and walked. Taken aback by what he saw, he fell to the spiked floor where his hands were pricked and the flaming soil squelched its thirst with his blood, he squinched at the smarting pain and got up again. Face to face was he now against the ancient crow, he could not estimate his living years but never has he seen the black bird with feathers so aged they had turned greyish. He had no eyes of his own, a blue zircon shone in his eye sockets, and they coruscated in the green mist like a deep blue azure sea surrounded by algae, the blind seers vision cut through the curling smoke rising into nothingness. A murder of crows stood and watched as their master spoke.

"Fear not, we shall not eat you. We find only the flesh of the dead appetizing, the far too gone, the unidentifiable and the defiled. If a pact is made beforehand, they will be revived, if not, their souls are of no concern nor of use to us, only their bodies."

"And you know what they say," said what seemed to be his second in command, "you are what you eat."

"You may be familiar with some of our handywork, your beloved king for example, he had come for our guidance once."

"The King deals with necromancy!" exclaimed Tobias.

"Yes indeed. I have commissioned the painting that hangs above his doors, the one he gazes at like a simpleton in a gallery, the only memory he could recall. They say memory maketh man, but I would not know. Murder and art, it gladdens me to say, are two things we excel at. Now tell me this, how old is the King? Think, torturer, think."

"He is a nonagrian, even more I believe."

"Yes, even more. How did he survive all these wars, why does he cower in his castle walls? Do you even wonder about those who rule over you?"

"It is not something I want to think about."

"Hah!" cawed the greater crow, the uncrowned king, "what else is there to think about? Money? We have seen you and the extension of your greed. You come to our council, but we do not serve your kind, we humiliate them, strip them from their rightful belongings including their own bodies, mortality matters, coin does not. Your God forgives, we are under no such obligation. Give us one good reason not to take your life."

He offered the golden rope as tribute, his hands open and his arms shivered beneath the weight as his slightly bended knees barely kept upright.

"And you would truly squander all your wealth to live a life as pathetic as yours?"

"Yes!" came an exclamation from his mouth, from unconvinced lips.

"That is odd, odd indeed. You were a man wishing for death not too long ago, a man like you should recompense all his wealth at our feet for a swift demise and yet you..."

"Yet I beg of you to let me go. I acknowledge the sudden change of heart and accept it wholeheartedly."

The crows laughed at Tobias, "fool, all the wealth you have amassed in no concern of ours, but no matter. Let it serve as a re-minder of its worthlessness. Guard!" he called for his crow, "throw this chain into the deepest pit you have ever known." A bird de-scended like a black cloud and before he knew it, a load had been lifted from the torturer's hands.

"What do I get in return?" he was afraid his question would be regarded as impertinence, but he spoke the words regardless.

"Do you want to live again after your death?"

"Why would I? I have no idea what to do with my time as it is."

"Ah yes, I have dealt with your kind before. The confused and the weary of existence. Why surrender when you still draw breath? It seems like asking circular defeatist questions that answer them-selves. If divorce exists, why marry? If failure exists, why try? And if death lurks around, why live? My dear boy, how are you going to spend your time? With nothing to do in life, time becomes too much no matter how little, and with something to do, all the time in the world is not enough. Finding an occupation, or a preoccupation in life is the entire meaning of existence. But do not listen to me, I deal with the dead not the living."

That strange man interfered lest he is forgotten, "I am the Count Kruger of Callistero, hear my words!"

"Oh!" the animal god mocked, "his majesty demands attention and he shall get it. I do remember you, I have eaten your kidney once, such sumptuous flesh. In earnest, I say this, 'Milord,' but I have always found your kind, the leaders of the human tribes far too flawed for me to grace them, but my mercy knows no bounds and my generosity abyssal, truly a bottomless pocket. Your kind are far too foolish; they fumble about, they confuse virtue with sins, pride with humility, greed with altruism, the upright with the crooked and yet we grant them a second chance, and even then, our gifts are squandered. Thankfully, most people see through the smoke screen and skullduggery, not that they would confront you, for in the presence of a liar, and in a house of lies, honesty is a sin. What do you want now, your 'majesty'?"

"I want all of my fallen troops to return so that we could have our revenge."

"Done. Now leave at once. Lest I peck your eyes out. God knows we want what we do not have, and I have always found the eyeballs the most tender of flesh. Succulent, beneath the glassy exterior lies a goo of meet pureed to perfection." The count paid one last apologetic glance at the way of the torturer and before he left, he whispered, "though they deal with metaphysics, they are still animals. If they have not granted you permission to leave, stand your ground." His statement was met with a nod, and the bitter feeling on his tongue, it was that of abandonment. Kruger left, behind him the murder of crows knew exactly what he said word for word and their beaks smiled at the irony of it all for they knew the ways of man and his brutality, as atrocious and savage as the animal kingdom.

"And what do you want, Tobias of Vorwahl?" asked the crow.

"My golden chain."

"Bah! It has not been a mere moment since your separation from it and you demand to be reunited. Very well, but I must say that the place you are headed to with us requires a pact from you. You shan't survive without it. You will die and be reborn."

"So be it."

"We usually would eat it when you have met death, but exceptions exist, and this instance shall be one such exception. What part would you like to sacrifice? Oh, I know, I would like your right eye. Yes, thine right eye is what I need, if given to me I shall grant you eternal life within a body that could withstand pain, dismemberment, hunger, and thirst. Yes, such a gift I would never grant, I give second chances but for you? For your right eye? I present to you eternity."

Tobias shuddered at the thought but stood his ground with a pasty white skin that cracked from the heat. He could not think much as terror had taken its toll. He was presented a blunt instrument, a twig from the euphorbia milli, to befoul the vision of the temple which was his body. If man had the image of God, the image would have been desecrated again and again. So be it, he thought, the nerves ached, and his body twitched in refusal to what his mind demanded, but it was unavailing for the ghost in the temple willed its own demise, and the temple, weak flesh and bones faltered in its ineffective protest. There can only be one god, and it was the coin, and it was in the coin. His view of the world was narrow, and now narrowed even further with his eye jumping out of its socket. He stood with blood pouring from an opening in his skull and one eye crying in pain, his body collapsed, both hands covered not the eye that he lost, but the one he still had.

"Good." The eye was served to him by a helper, "now follow my servant, he will show you the way." The black figure flew, and the torturer recollected himself in seeking his rightful fortune. He denied death as he rode on his horse, he did not feel any different now, no superhuman strength whatsoever, just pain, lasting and everlasting. His one eye oscillated between the two tasks at hand, looking upward towards his guide, and looking downwards in order not to fall into some fiery pit, but it failed, and he and his horse did fall in a crack in the earth. He did not see where the beyond boiling temperature picked the flesh clean from his bones, but he felt it all; his fall, his death, and his rebirth. He pulled himself from the fire and walked the earth again with his scarred flesh naked with a few melted pieces of metal burned into his skin. He did not know how to feel. He was now an abomination.

"Come, quick! I do not have all day," cawed his impatient partner. Without a word, he followed on foot. His immortality had given him thoughts he never had, those of godhood, those who made the everyman tremble in his boots, how many kingdoms could he acquire, how many wars to emerge victorious from, how many harems he could claim, and how much gold, oh, mountains and mountain chains of gold glimmering and shining to the ends of the earth. He smiled now. His worries left him in shambles, but he was reforged in the fire, he now had optimism, speculation, and plans of domination.

"Here it is," claimed the crow, "it is here that I have dropped your chain. Now go and wrap it around your neck again."

"And how do I know that thou art telling the truth? 'Tis a pit too deep, one cannot see the end of it."

"I shall give you a torch," the crow left and came back with a torch in his beak. The man handled it in his hand and dropped it carefully so that on its downward trajectory it won't hit the floors. The torch still burned, and he beheld his chain, long and golden inhabiting the deep dark floor.

"I have one last demand."

"Indeed, for I shall listen to you no more. What is it that you need?"

"A rope to climb back up. And a nail, of course."

"Agreed," the crow left and came back with a rope and a nail. The man nailed one end of it securely to the ground, and the other end suspended to the dark downward depth. He checked the firmness of the nail in the ground and the structural soundness of the rope, it was all well as far as he was concerned. Before he could dismiss his companion, he was already on his way with his back turned and wings defying gravity. It seemed to him that there a fault in his reality where he was bound, no matter who accompanied him, to be left on his lonesome. Jumping from the edge of the precipice, he dropped into the abyss, leaping downwards for he knew he would revive himself as if nothing had happened. It would take minutes; what seemed to be an eternity and fear was making its way to his heartbeat and blood flow like a sickness even when his mind was reassuring itself that there was nothing to fear. It took an hour to reach his chain as he descended in freefall, every bone in his body broke beyond repair upon impact, from the calcaneus to his skull, his skin tore, and his flesh and blood made a puddle in which he lay momentarily, and it happened again. He felt it all; his death and resurrection, and despite the pain that passed, a smile was drawn on his face. He held the bloodied chain in his hands and kissed it again and again until it was tired of his lips. He held the rope in his hand and pulled himself upwards but with a few pulls he had dropped to his back and the flying nail laid next to his face as the rest of the rope dwindled down, so slowly it descended as if time had come to a standstill. He was not realizing the gravity of the situation before, but it was then that his eyes opened wide, and his pupils dilated in fear. No, he screamed to himself, in his mind or at the tip of his tongue, it did not matter, for there was no one to listen and no difference would have been made. He was left with his maddening screams, begging mercy, and cursing the powers that be. He tried to climb. He tried to hang himself amongst other ways of taking his own life, but nothing would happen. Nothing would happen, he could deny his end for he could still draw breath, but the pit was the end of him, and he was left to live a life of death. He hungered but did not starve. He thirsted but could not quench. He lived but he could not die.

Within the walls of Callistero, funeral rites and processions were interrupted by the dead. Upon the arrival of the Count, there was a shift in reality; one in which many would deny what they saw to maintain their sanity, even if it meant the denial of the deceiving senses. But there was no deception, the dead had returned. The Count came back and on his command his legions rose from their eternal slumber which he interrupted. The people fled in fear, Was this the prophesied end? Would the living God return now? Amidst the chaos, it was hard to know; tables were being turned, the bodies in the wheelbarrows removed themselves and their handlers ran, cowered, or covered their eyes and slowly backed away. One would hear glass breaking, doors opening and closing, and footsteps of people fleeing. The widowed women who yearned to see their men again now fled for their lives, forlorn fathers and mothers would approach the risen bodies of the fallen soldiers, but the men seldom knew them; those who did were given their preferred memory by the crows and it would include their caretakers, otherwise everything and everyone else was forgotten. "Rise, my legions, there is an impostor among us. He had taken my army, he had taken my wife, my kingdom, and my very own life. Rise, the grave can wait." They knew that voice, and they knew the man, some memories were stronger than death. They ambushed the stables and stole the horses, some others walked, all had marched behind their count seeking their former glory.

The Countess and her lover were nowhere to be seen within the city walls. Upon further inspection and inquiry in the castle, Alice the servant confessed that Claire and her lover were long gone. the constable had taken the army and marched towards Vorwahl to end the reign of Edward once and for all. It was foolish, he thought, foolish on two accounts: taking a woman, and a member of loyalty to the frontlines of battle, and facing the fearsome Edward directly. He divided his men, those without horses were to stay and defend the city from any possible attacks, and the others were to join him. He marched, like a wildfire spread in the wind with speed and ferocity unseen. The man was vicious in battle. He craved battle. He lived to kill and anticipated death with wide open arms, and that is exactly the reason why Krill thought he had to go. He had to kill him in order for the kingdom to prosper, so he went in the dead of the night and slit his throat in his own bed, the bed in which the constable would sleep on, the bed whose covers and sheets would not rid of the dried blood of their rightful owner. There was no uproar after the murder. Loyalty in warfare is not to the man; loyalty is to the rank and the banner, the men who accompanied the returned warrior were the men who had their loyalty misplaced to their leader. Revenge had finally come, it was within reach, and in his anticipation, he could feel his heart beat faster, he could hear his blood pumping in his heart and his head, and his tinnitus ringing in his ears as a reminder of the clashing metal and cannonballs plowing his men into the ground and levitating them in pieces to places far away, though at times the human body seemed firm in its structure where everything in it respective place played a pivotal role, with human ingenuity it did not take much to rip it apart. His sights were set to Vorwahl, but his mind and his heart to revenge.

The betrayer was now in sight. They have caught the escaped lovers and their cavalry by their side on the outskirts of Vorwahl before they could reach and besiege its walls. They halted. Both of them witnessed their hearts drop for different reasons; Claire for the fact that she was caught with another man, or perhaps for the fact that her dead husband was alive, and Krill for seeing the man whose throat he cut riding a horse and getting closer to him, there was also the matter of him taking his wife as his soon to be betrothed. It was a muddled affair, one would know what to feel with things he is familiar with; those stranger occurrences were met with stranger feelings, a mixture of surprise, astonishment, fear, anger, and maybe a pinch of delight seeing a familiar sight. They would not know; they did not know what to say or what to feel and what to think and sat in their respective places ordering the men to stop in their tracks. No sound was made from the opposing parties, and the living feared the dead for they had not yet seen what follows, judgement, reincarnation, or nothingness, and in a way, they were not looking forward to it. Too much harm has been done, to them and by them.

"I see you have taken my wife as a mistress," spoke the Count, "I wonder, dear wife of mine, what it feels like to betray, a thing I have never done. At worst, you conspire against me. At best, you are as much a victim of circumstance and trickery as I am. I demand you to return to castle, we shall discuss this all soon enough."

"You were supposed to be dead! I need to know what is happening, and I am not leaving before knowing. Please, please explain," she begged, looking into Krill's eyes, pulling his disbelieving face towards her own as they were still on horseback, then she looked at her husband, "I shall not budge, and you have no power over me."

"Very well, wife dearest. Your claim on authority is questionable at best, but if I do not have power over you, you forget that I have power over a hundred other men. Before your dogs are let loose in your defense, think about the lives you are responsible for taking. As for you gentlemen, I want what you want, to save the damsel and kill the villain." The end of his sword pointed towards Krill. "I challenge you a duel. There is no need for further bloodshed, do you not all agree? There is no need for many to die for the sin of one man."

The soldiers stepped away from the Constable. Kruger's men took his wife back with no resistance from their opposition. Krill remained silent. He descended from his horse as his enemies took his beloved from him. They placed her gently into a carriage despite her incessant pleading and went off with her as she cried bitter tears of sadness, even beyond that, tears of betrayal and confusion for she would not know who to blame, her lover or her own self. She looked back to see the duel had already commenced. "Whoever wins," she thought to herself as she saw her lovers duel, "I am the one at loss." She would beg them to stop but the distance between them grew too far, but not far enough not to see what was happening. Her loved one fell dead, and another blow delivered a murderous thrust by the jagged edge of the rusted sword through his suffocating chest, a strike she could feel in her very own bosom with senses ululating within her. She wept. Her protests and caterwauling went unnoticed by the coachman and little by little her cries grew silent with the absolute taking over of melancholy, her happily ever after was cut short in its duration and her travel to the comfort of her home did not bring joy but sorrow. She could not walk in her state, some henchmen carried her to her prison of a home and laid her on her bed, and a table beneath her held above it a bouquet of wilted lilies bent in a vase filled with mildewy, unchanged water.

The armies stood in a defensive state awaiting to clash but with their leaders gone they stood like a decapitated body; there were no orders to await, and the second in command did not say a word. In his heart, he thought their king sacrificed himself to save the rest of them and he himself left not out of cowardice but rather out of gratitude, if they fought and more soldiers' lives were claimed, his death would be in vain, and with his departure the rest of the army dispersed.

Chapter Twelve

THE KING IS DEAD

Violent convulsions set the kings heart beating to an arrhythmic spasmic beat and his mind shattered to a thousand different places yet could not think a single coherent thought. He wrote wordless sentences in his mind and painted formless images. His past haunted his present and halted his future. He was young when he was coronated as king, young indeed. It was mere days after his twelfth birthday, a year since his mother had passed away and a lifetime since his father had left them to their own devices. He was still the head of the house in a way, for he ruled over the kingdom itself and all people were his subjects. He would never visit, nor would he send someone to see if they fared well in the harshest of winters. He did not intervene when his mother got sick. He did not attend her funeral when she died. He did not leave a note, nor send a kind word his way. One day, the roof collapsed over his head and the King did not move a bone in his finger to command the best builders. He had to renovate, for the King knew everything and knew about this very particular mishappening but cared for no one, not even his blood, it seemed. No fire would keep the young Edward warm, not even the one that raged in his faint heart. He was neglected by God and man, his heavenly father and his earthly one. He was taking his last dying breath and he knew it. He breathed in the reapers kiss and cuddled in his boney caress. Before he would leave this mortal coil of toil and pain, a crow came to him, in his craven, squeamish self he retreated in his own skin knowing there was no escape and nowhere to disappear. The azure eyes shone brightly in the glittering raindrops, colder than ice they descended, and every drop burned in his skin until it turned from pale white to blue; his day has come and he knew. The crow consoled him and offered him a chance to return once again to this life. All he wanted was a piece of his flesh, for he was famished in the desolate, barren winter, or so he had claimed. A silent pact was made, and the scared young child lost his pinky, a small price to pay it was, especially since he did not feel a part in his body. After the crow had feasted, he asked the child, "if one memory you like burned into your brain, which one would it be?" The child answered, "this very moment. Nothing of worth came before, and I deny all that shall come afterwards."

The child slept all winter, and in the summer, he arose from his grave, took a bath, and stole some clean clothes. He relished in the fact that no one had known him, it was to his advantage given his clandestine activities and proclivities. He snuck into the chambers of his father, the King, and while he and his queen slept, he drew a knife but could not kill them. He slept in the darkest parts, the unlit corners and corridors robbing the leftovers from the kitchen and bathing when the help did not look. He ate like royalty but slept like a thief, with one eye or both eyes open and a consciousness ready to flee at any time. Seasons would pass and he would live like a rat within the castle halls until one day the King would address his people from the balcony, and in their fury, they would not hear a word, and in broad daylight, with roars of the maddening crowd, he drew his dagger and thrust it in the King's groin and he would slash away as much flesh as he could off the bone as the King called him "son" and begged him to stop without fighting back. It was a bloody affair, and one would think it would be met with disgust and loud reprimands by the crowd, but they rejoiced. They proclaimed that such a brave kid would not have a hair on his head touched as punishment, for once the people were in your favor, no opposing force would ever be formidable, and it did not matter if you were right or wrong, moral matters would only be discussed after the fact, if ever. What is right is what the crowd thinks is right, such was the law of the revolution. The remaining royal family was exiled, and the commoners took over the castle, until Edward grew from his tender years. In his delusion, he had planted the thought like a cursed seed in his head; the thought that he was the rightful heir, royal blood flowed within him, and the people did wrong to his family and should have punished him for murdering royalty but instead, they revered him and celebrated his darkest hour. He would put their good will to good use, and in a moonless night all the commoners in the castle he would slay, he scoured the upper parts, the lower parts, the spiral staircases, the cellar, the stables, and the forbidden rooms. Every inch he would look for the unwanted, for the common wretch, and he would end their lives.

A battle would be fought afterwards by their families, if mercy begets mercy, blood begets blood. The king would search high and low for people who were loyal to the monarchy even after they were gone, and to his surprise they were aplenty. He gathered all the able-bodied men he could find and secured a victory to himself and to his bloodline as it were. But after his victorious days, nights came with all its questions and doubts, who was he loyal to? What was the point in all the bloodshed? Did he really care about victory? What about his slain family? "Slain family! Gah!" he exclaimed. His family was his mother, like a Greek demigod, he was a man divided, the part that mattered to him was the divine, and the divine had a breast, one he suckled at her bosom when he was toothless and weak. That was the part that mattered; the part that made his bed and cleaned his clothes, the one that tended to his wounds, physical and mental, the one who never complained despite the hardship she faced for she knew complaining was a first step in announcing defeat. That part, the divine part, was dead. What would she want? He did not know, he did not know, nor could he remember her now. It tore him to pieces. The faceless mother, in remembrance of her silhouette, he turned to more lachrymose thoughts. He knew of her the way a stranger has heard a tale about some person or another, he would try to reminisce, but the only picture his mind could produce was that of his flesh falling piece by piece in the cold as he stood having the ability to do nothing. Indeed, all he could remember was a picture and thoughts of hatred and cruelty, he would wrong the world in its entirety as the world had entirely wronged him.

He stood victorious over mountains and mountains worth of corpses. For a century, he had triumphed, and his ego silently grew in volume. Even if he was to die at any given moment, he had rest assured that he had made his way into a hall of history where tales of his magnanimity and horribleness would be told until the end of time, men of the future would sympathize with him as a product of his time, that somehow the past is an excuse for his madness, and on the other side of the crowd, are those who would deny his greatness and highlight his cruelty. He did not care. The words of lesser men in any given time mattered not. He felt something, was it remorse? No, 'twas anger; nothing but silent anger, at himself, at his predecessor, and at the world and its creator. A regicide, a king slayer, and a kin slayer. A good king, a horrible king, a tyrant, a warmonger, and a peacekeeper, he has been all, and he has been none, all these things he was under the same name, Edward. When the people spoke of Edward, what did they say? It did not matter to him. The past was worthless, especially one he could not remember.

Larson came back after perilous journeys to a place far away; a place where men forgot what it was to live. They forgot the immense worth of beauty, romance, godliness, and goodness. It was all lost on them. They barbarically swung swords and their intent was not to merely hurt but kill by any means necessary. If anyone was to return from such flights, it would be him, the prized procession, the king of messengers. To his most pleasant surprise, he had found Sue, her young ones by her side, and his brother! Oh how he missed his brother, and he knew he was also missed for their relationship was formed on mutuality of everything, respect, love, and even sacrifice. They greeted each other with an infinitesimal display of care for one another, but the smiles they had on their faces spoke volumes; some things go without saying, and where words are not wanted, they are not needed. He had noticed the change in the family; they seemed stranger than when they have embarked on their journey. It was normal for the adventurer to return differently, but there was something peculiar about them. It would all be revealed to him as Sue made her announcement.

"We have not returned for the sake of returning, but rather to bid you farewell. We owe you one last goodbye."

"What on earth do you mean? Where to? You cannot possibly leave for good!" exclaimed Larson.

"Are you mad?" asked simply the eldest, Melvin, in great disappointment.

"And where are your golden feathers?" asked Susan.

"We have gotten rid of them. We are going to join our wild brothers and sisters."

"You cannot..." Melving choked on his words, "you cannot possibly think this is the right thing to do. Have you given it enough thought? You are aware after all the hardships and diffi-culties that nature has to offer! Within the human realm, we are safe from most harm, we live longer and happier, it is only in case of exceptions that we suffer from their hands, meanwhile nature is cruel without mercy, our children die from unknown illnesses, disasters, and predators, amongst other things, not to mention the lack of hygiene. Please, you must see reason!"

"We have made a decision, and we made it unanimously as a family. It is out of goodwill that we have returned to say our good-byes, but we do not owe you an explanation."

Larson took a few steps towards the door, "I shall be right back; I have a message to deliver to the King and afterwards we shall speak. Until then, I urge you not to leave, at least not until we talk about this."

Nelson nodded.

Larson flew and sat on the King's lap; his most prized posses-sion. He handed him a letter from the war-torn lands. It bore bad news, and the bearer of bad news sat still on his lap. The war was over and there was no reason to rejoice for the King had lost. He had been finally defeated. His trickery had come to an end and po-tentially so had his reign. His silence was not peaceful, wedged in his throne he was immobile, unmoving yet if he willed it, he would annihilate all that existed around him. There was no expression to discern on his face, did that letter spell his downfall? How would anyone know? No other eyes had read the scroll and there was no reason to conjecture. He was befuddled, how could he lose? Every move was calculated, deduced through abductive logic and mathematical reasoning. It would take a mi...miracle? No, miracles do not exist, not to him even if he was brought back from the dead, there was reason for it. Maybe it was all a dream, including this very moment. He held Larson in his hands as if to console him, each wing he grabbed between the index fingers and the thumbs of his respective hands, and he tore the wings from his body without warning. Blood fountained from the separation, it was not long before the messenger hemorrhaged and collapsed dead at once.

Word spread fast within castle walls. The caretaker entered his quarters mourning in a way he had never before and the birds jumped around in curiosity, what happened? Where is our king, our leader? Melvin flew from the pen and returned with eyes wide open from the horror he had witnessed. It took him long to gather around the tribe and tell of his most gruesome finding. Between disorder and melancholy, their wings flapped. They all followed one another and gathered again under the tree, their haven from man.

"I know our loss is immensurable, but," Nelson spoke.

"Silence!" interrupted the elder, "you break the commands of the goddess and man with your dreams and tall tales of freedom. How do we know that this punishment is not godsent because of your insolence?"

"We are called to uphold the commands of the goddess, and in doing so no harm is supposed to befall us. Why then does misfortune make its way to our very home? We have broken the commands of man in straying from the pen, that much is true, but never have we ever opened a sealed letter, yet Larson dies."

"You make a good point," replied he sullenly, "as for the rest of you, I know you look to me for guidance, but I am as lost as you are. We shall not return to our home as it is now a house of horror, I do not wish to see the image of the dead king in my mind ever again."

"Then come with us," Sue's motion jerked as she wished to look the tribe in their eyes, "all of you, I beg you, we are born to be free. Cast away the golden fetters, surely you will bleed at first but after that you are free."

They have aided each other from the chains that bound them in servitude for man and proclaimed freedom. They flew with the dispersed winds and united in the tree where their kind lived blissfully with nature, as one. Communalities did not change, their family was now extended, and tales grew in multitudes, but Susan, her husband, and her daughter were left behind on their own terms. They refused to join the crowd, but they also refused to return to the castle.

"Can you fly? Can you fly my heart, my cornerstone, the marrow of my bone?"

"Yes mother, where to?" Her sullen countenance was obvious to the eye; she had recovered but barely.

"Let them go to their kind, but I am most accustomed to the ways of man, the comfort of man, and the medicine of man, and I know a place far away where only learned men of letters stay. Let us leave to them at once and seek haven among them."

They made their way through the cloudless sky where their only companions were the alien things that peaked through the window of our world; the sun, the stars, the moon, and the heavens kept them company when all things on earth conspired against them, or so it seems ever since a messenger was murdered.

The King did not care that much. He did not care about the bird. He did not care about men. He did not care about God, and to a degree, apathy was embedded to the point of disregarding his own self. Nothing mattered now, it was a few moments before he would be captured and killed by the many enemies he had made. Julian would humiliate him before killing him. He could flee of course, but no, he wanted punishment, the feeling of pain, and death. Days would pass and he would do nothing but relish in the fact that he is king. He would bask in the shrinking glory like an ocean facing an incoming drought. His meandering tears and lack of hydration shrunk him to a lake, then a puddle. He would wait, fasting without a drop of water, nor the slightest bit of bread, he would do penance for nothing and no one. It was time now; he could hear the enemy. He stood on his balcony atop of his hill and commiserated in the fact that his end was near. It would be better, he thought, for everyone, including himself. The small heads and shrunken ponies grew to be fearsome soldiers and beastly horses surrounding the castle gates. His guards wanted to fight but he prohibited them, the gates were open, and enemies barged in without the most miniscule of resistance, the people of the city stood outside their homes as they welcomed the strangers but weary from their existence, for the fates of the people are often intertwined and unilateral to the fate of their royalty, like a head and its body.

"Fear not, I have come for your king. You shan't suffer for his sake," spoke King Julian in his carriage. He knew there was no need for his armor and steed. He wore a mantle, a silken threaded suit, a thing one would wear to church or to dine with the finest aristocracies in the lands. There was no fight, and that much was obvious to all. They accepted him as a new king and greeted him as such. In seeing them cheer on his archnemesis, Edward felt betrayal, a betrayal he had foreseen, one he agreed to for he knew he had as much a role to play in it as the people did. Leading the convoy was a face they could not recognize but, in a way, knew. It was the sorrowful mercenary, Margaret led the invading convoy, and she was disappointed with the lack of battle, but she did not mind. It was easier to get her target this way with as little resistance as possible. The people gathered from far and wide, it was very seldom that justice would be served in such rawness, such nakedness as to know what it really was. Justice was revenge.

The priests who vowed piety to God also vowed loyalty to the monarch. They lied on both occasions, and they were the first to gather with the angry crowd. They declared that they would read his death sentence, and they would pray for God to have mercy on his soul as they took it upon themselves to take his life. The executioner walked with them, and without any bindings, walked freely Jeremiah. He beseeched the people, but his words were unheard noise. The captured king was stripped naked; his garment torn to pieces in the hands of the rabid crowd, his mantle fragmented into little threads in furious hands who put in their empty pockets invisible atoms of its color, and his crown was stomped on, its golden gallantry depredated by the marauders. It lost its shine, blackened by the soot and the scratches, until it was broken to pieces then collected by those who scurried around the stampeding feet with a hawk's eye to identify the tawdry looking blackened jewels that fell off it. There was nothing on his body to signify his superior status now, yet their humiliation ritual was not complete, now that his soul was scarred, his body came next. They clawed on the skin until his flesh was shown, bruises and scars and tattooed palms reddened on his skin. Now, there was nothing left. They had to dispose of him properly, they had to burn him.

They built a stake and tied him to it as Jeremiah ran about the crowd like an ant. He would beg them to stop, and they would threaten him into silence with violence. He could not reason with the wrathful zeitgeist. He was ignored, and in realizing he could do nothing he ran to the victim of all the violence and sat by his side. He saw the cold gnawing at him, he was shivering, and his mouth moved and produced vapors but no words he spoke. Without thought, the priest gave him the upper part of the bear skin garment and covered what he could of his body.

"Leave. Leave me, old man. I cannot repay you, and I refuse to die with debts. I have wronged you. I have condemned you to die."

"You do not condemn people, you fool. God does."

"Cold. So cold."

"Collect yourself. Collect yourself and pray, your time has come."

"I see this as a will of God."

"Nay. Wrath is a deadly sin, God does not will sin but man in his free will more often than none will seek out sin deliberately."

"What will become of me, father?"

"It is not for men to say, but I will pray for you."

"After all I have done?"

"Because of what you have done."

"I wish you were near me when I needed you the most when I was neglected by God and man. Where were you? I died from the cold, and in a dream a crow visited me, he promised me power beyond compare. Power to rise from death. I do not care if it was superstition, and I do not care if in reality I did not die, all physical phenomenon you could discern for a scientific reason. I swear it had happened. I died before."

"The cold is making you see things."

"Perhaps."

There was silence as the priest's old, wrinkled fingers moved along the rosary from bead to bead. In the background was a deafening roar that came from a lion's den, but it was the sounds of men.

"What will eternity think of me, father?"

"Think nothing of it, for it will think nothing of you."

"Just like that?"

"It takes a successful man to blame his shortcomings on himself, a failure blames the rest of the world. You had the makings of greatness at times, but you squandered them." The old man spoke silently, there was nothing more he could say or do. The punished king said his last words, privately to the priest but loud enough so the public could hear. He knew those were his last words.

"Do you know why I have never taken up a wife? It was not out of altruism or a sense of duty to the people that I had no family nor children of my own, I had no ulterior motives. I knew you were a thankless lot. What would I bring kids for, for you to slaughter like sheep? I would never be as heartless and cruel as to pass on a life as dreary as this one to a thing as helpless as a child. Burn me, maggots, set me ablaze, see this through to the end."

"And we shall," spoke Cecil. The stake was loaded with dry twigs and branches ready to be burned, but Jeremiah resisted, he would not leave his side. It took ten men to remove him. He kept his gaze fixated at the king's eyes as he was carried away in defeat. Before the torch would be dropped, Margaret made haste to the man in ropes and pieced his heart with a dagger. It was not out of mercy, but hatred, she would not let someone claim his life. The King died before the fire ate his body like a Roman candle, and his portrait burned as it hung on the walls. The crowd finally knew who the King was looking at. The King who had lived his entire life outside of war in a dimly lit hall overlooking the people, died beneath them in a bright fire.

The weeping Jeremiah was carried outside of the castle gates and thrown to survive on his own devices in his semi-nakedness. He prayed ceaselessly until the cold claimed his life once and for all.

Chapter Thirteen
HAPPILY EVER AFTER

The feathered wings came together in a grand circle as they nested in the tree. Death will haunt them now. Predators surrounded them around every corner and there was no medicine to heal their ailments, but never were they happier than they were now. There was time to mourn the loss of Larson, but soon life would move on as it always did. They would adapt in no time. Melvin would boost the morale in camp, convincing himself that this was a better life, for the first step in convincing others was in convincing oneself.

"Brothers and sisters, our ancestors have traded pain for luxury and hardship for ease, all at the cost of their freedom. We shall reconvey our freedom no matter the cost. They were slaves with feathers of gold, but we here are free, we are where we rightfully belong, and so make this place a rightful home, for you and those who shall follow in your steps."

The pigeons cheered on their sage.

"Mother what happened to the kings, the ones you were telling us a story about? Do they live happily ever after? Does the war end?" asked Rosy in anticipation for her finale.

"I do not know, my dearest. I do not know, and I wish I did not care. But enough about that, let the worries of men worry men alone. Our story ends now, and it shall begin again some other day. Let us sleep now, our days shall grow longer in toil, but we work together, and things will be easier for us all."

Rosy nodded, the little birds warmed up beneath the guarding wings of their mother and their father. Despite his loss, Nelson was happier than he has ever been reunited with his family.

Chapter Fourteen

CUCKOO FROM A BIRD'S EYE VIEW

After days of travel with her daughter, Susan arrived at the prestigious university of Vardinberg where Callum and Robert Ebert were discussing their manuscript with Mr. Mime. The poor farmer was at loss for words with joy, his wife was finally pregnant. He did not care whether the baby turned out to be boy or girl, both were equally a blessing from the lord, he could not contain his happiness. They begged him to focus as the couple needed to finish the book before its deadline on midnight tonight or else all their work would have to be rewritten for some other audience.

"Just in the nick of time the bird descends. Ask her of all the details that you might have missed from that day," Callum begged.

"Quickly lad, we do not have time," Robert pulled his hair as stress silently claimed years of his life.

The interrogation with the animal happened, it was most fruitful as they offered her fruits. In finalizing their words before they would publish their manuscript, they asked Mr. Mime,

"And are you certain that this little bird, the one that sits on your shoulder, whispered all of this to you?"

"She," he looked around hesitantly before his voice dropped a few octaves, "she would have if I understood a word she said."

Printed in the United States
by Baker & Taylor Publisher Services